Guardians Of The Round Table 2
Goblin Boots

Guardians Of The Round Table 2
Goblin Boots

Avril Sabine, Storm Petersen
and Rhys Petersen

Cracked Acorn Productions
Australia

Guardians Of The Round Table 2: Goblin Boots

Published by

Cracked Acorn Productions

PO Box 1365

Gympie, Queensland 4570

Australia

978-1-925617-67-2 (Kindle)

978-1-925617-68-9 (EPUB)

978-1-925617-69-6 (Print)

Genre: Young Adult Fantasy LitRPG

Cover design by Caitlyn Petersen

For those who love side quests and are always distracted by them.

**When all actions have repercussions,
it isn't really agame.**

Returning to Inadon, Mallory and her companions are determined to level up, gain better gear and learn new abilities. They soon discover it might be more difficult than they realise when they encounter members of the dark forces. Will their actions have the wrong consequences or will they have time to gain the experience points they need before they become a target of the dark forces?

*

This story was written by Australian authors using Australian spelling.

Name Pronunciation

Like many names there is more than one way to pronounce the following ones. These are the pronunciations used in this story.

Characters

Ahron (ah-ron)

Danae (da-nay)

Grotmur (grot-mer)

Kruth (kr-uth)

Sarisa (sa-risa)

Places

Buckneth (buck-neth)

Eridell (air-a-dell)

Inadon (in-ah-don)

Shadhurst (shad-hurst)

Simria (sim-re-ah)

Surith (soo-rith)

Ursen (ur-sen)

Wildebay (wild-bay)

Foreword

Opening stats, Mallory's notebook entries recapping the previous adventures and other details can be found at:

www.avrilsabine.com/series/gotrt

The notebook entries will contain spoilers if you haven't read the book they refer to.

Chapter One

Mallory put her soft leather boots, which were in a plastic bag, into her backpack. The disc was already in there and she glanced around her bedroom, trying to think of anything else she might need. She wore jeans, a t-shirt, a long sleeve shirt over her t-shirt and she'd tucked her woollen socks inside her boots. She'd had lunch a bit over an hour ago and tied her brown hair, which was naturally streaked with copper highlights, back into a plait. She wasn't about to have it tangled and knotted like last time. Her gaze stopped on the notebook she'd bought while they'd been out earlier. After they'd talked to Dorset, Richelle and Jed. The notebook was lying on her bed, a pen beside it, the purple fake leather cover blending with her bedspread. Grabbing them, she shoved both into her backpack. Now she had everything. She hoped.

Taking a deep breath, she picked up her backpack,

a shiver of excitement rushing through her. They were about to return to Inadon. She could almost feel the dagger in her hand, a wand in the other. "Journal." She whispered the word, but nothing happened. Soon it would. She'd only have to think the word and she'd be able to check her stats, quests, a map of the areas she'd travelled and notes.

There was a banging on her door. "What's taking you so long?" Brodie demanded.

She opened the door, grinning at the impatient look her brother gave her. He was sixteen, a year younger than her, with green eyes that were identical to her own and short brown hair. She eyed the backpack he carried. It looked full. "We can't take anything other than what we wear." She kept her voice low, not wanting their mum, who was in the lounge room at the other end of the hallway watching a movie, to hear.

"It's food."

"You can't take it with you."

Brodie grinned. "I can if it's in my stomach."

She followed him along the hallway, slowly shaking her head. If the backpack was full of food he'd end up making himself sick eating all of it before they left.

Norine looked up from the television. "I want the

pair of you back in time for dinner. I don't see why you couldn't play your computer game here. I'll be finished with the TV in a few minutes."

"They've been over here every day this week. It's our turn to go to their place," Brodie said.

"This better not be a new game. I was serious about you not buying any more games until your school results improve."

"We've already told you, Mum. The game Brodie brought home Wednesday was mine. He took it off me at the bus stop. It wasn't like Mrs Torres could tell who it belonged to," Mallory said. "Brodie was annoyed that I could buy a game and he couldn't."

"As if I've got the money to buy games anyway," Brodie muttered.

Mallory barely managed to keep a straight face. He had more money than he'd normally have. All he'd spent his earnings from their last lot of questing on had been a school shirt. One he'd managed to pick up secondhand. "We're going next door to play my game, Mum. I've finally convinced Brodie to play RPGs." This time she did grin. Technically it was her game. Or at least her game disc. And she was the party leader. Much to her brother's disgust.

"You've both done your homework?" Norine looked from one to the other.

"How many times have you got to ask?" Brodie demanded. "Yes already."

"We've both done our homework and we'll be back before dinner." Mallory strode towards the door, glancing over her shoulder. "Well before dinner." Again she grinned. It was true. No matter how long they ended up staying on Inadon, they'd be reinserted back into this world only seconds after they'd left it. There was no way they'd be late for dinner. Even if there was a glitch it'd only mean a couple of minutes had passed. She slipped her feet into her sneakers that were by the door. "See you later."

"Both of you behave," Norine called out before they stepped outside, closing the door.

"Does killing wolves count as behaving?" Brodie asked softly, grinning at Mallory.

She tried not to laugh, especially after her mum's last comment. Her mum was sure to think the laughter was a reply and call them back to find out what they were up to. She managed to suppress her laughter, not speaking until they were nearly next door. "Were you trying to get us in trouble?"

"As if. I want to return to Inadon as much as you." Brodie raised his hand to knock on the door of the house next door.

There were very little differences between this

house and theirs. The entire block was filled with almost identical looking houses, the developer having used the same house plan, occasionally flipping it so that the lounge room was on the left-hand side of the house instead of the right like theirs and Ryan's home. The owners of the various houses in the neighbourhood personalised them through colour schemes, landscaping and adding a carport on one side. Neither of their houses had a carport.

Ryan opened the door before Brodie managed to knock. "What took you so long?" His black hair was tied at the nape of his neck and his dark brown eyes roamed Mallory's face. "Was there a problem?" He had on the shirt he'd worn to Inadon last time, a tear in the right sleeve and one in the side, a black t-shirt visible through the tear.

Mallory stepped close, sliding her arms around Ryan's waist. "I don't think Mum likes us spending time together." She glanced at Brodie who pushed past them to head inside. "Even with our siblings as chaperones."

Ryan chuckled, lowering his head to kiss her before drawing her inside and pulling the door closed. "It's only been a few days. Give her a chance to get used to it." He linked his fingers through hers, walking towards his bedroom. It was at the other end of the hallway on the right, in the same location as Mallory's. "Callum is trying to figure out what time we'll arrive. I left him muttering in my room and scribbling down his calculations."

"What has he come up with?" She tried to walk softly, not wanting to catch the attention of Ryan's parents and slow down their return to Inadon. It was impossible to be silent on wooden floorboards when wearing sneakers. Nor were Ryan's boots silent.

Ryan shrugged. "Callum's still working it out. He said if we leave this arve at two-thirty it will be about seventy hours since we were last there. I considered helping him with the calculations, but thought it'd give him something to do other than check out the front door to see if you pair were on your way over."

She grinned. "Is that so he didn't get in the way of you checking?"

Ryan laughed, but gave no answer.

Mallory entered Ryan's bedroom, her gaze travelling over everything, hearing Ryan close the door behind her. She'd only been in his room a couple of times. The curtains were drawn, the light was on and music played in the background. Unlike their house, that had carpet in the bedrooms, Ryan's room had the same timber flooring as the lounge room and hallway. Callum sat in the middle of the queen-sized bed, scribbling on a notepad and frowning, the black doonah rumpled and creased. He had the same brown eyes and black hair as his brother, but his was kept short, and at two years younger than Ryan he was the same age as Mallory. Where his brother was more solidly built, he was lanky.

Callum looked up, his frown clearing. "If we leave at two-thirty, we should reach Inadon about nine-forty in the evening. Give or take a few minutes. Not even a day will have passed."

"Should we wait so we'll arrive at daylight?" Mallory let go of Ryan's hand to take off her backpack.

Callum shook his head. "It'd take three days our time. I worked out a few conversions. Twenty-four hours here on Earth is four hours on Inadon. One week here is twenty-eight hours over there. For us to have a full day pass on Inadon it'll take six days here. And if we want to return to Inadon after a week has passed there, it'll take forty-two days here."

Chapter Two

Mallory stared at Callum. "Forty-two days." Surely that couldn't be right.

Callum nodded. "We're better off going and camping out somewhere while we wait for daylight. It'll be quicker."

"I'm not tired." Brodie set his backpack on the timber floor and took out a lunchbox, opening the lid to reveal a sandwich.

Mallory got her boots out of her backpack, dropping her mobile phone inside it since she couldn't take it with her, and sat beside Callum to exchange the boots for her sneakers. "We have a lantern. Maybe we could do something instead of sleeping."

"Isn't night meant to be better for fishing?" Callum set the notepad and pen aside.

Mallory finished pulling on her boots. "I have no

idea. I've never been fishing before." She took her pen, notebook and the disc out of her backpack. "I've never been interested in going fishing."

"Some fish are nocturnal." Ryan took the disc Mallory handed him, inserting it in his laptop.

Having finished the sandwich, Brodie grabbed a tub of yoghurt from his backpack and opened it. "We could have fish for breakfast." He looked at the yoghurt. "I didn't bring a spoon." He shrugged before raising the container to his mouth.

"You are going to make yourself sick." Mallory opened her notebook to the first page.

"Or make us sick from watching you," Callum said.

Ryan chuckled at Callum's comment before looking towards Mallory. "I think you need to put the disc in. It's coming up blank for me."

"One sec. What should I write in the notebook? Other than we're meant to be back for dinner and your parents are going out tonight."

Ryan shrugged. "I have no idea. Do you think this is necessary? It's not like we forgot anything last time we came back. And we don't plan to stay too long at a time. At least not until we can afford potions so we don't appear to age too fast for this world."

"I forgot about taking the rubbish out," Callum

said. "I would have been grounded if you hadn't reminded me."

"We don't have to worry about anything like that," Ryan said. "Put the disc in."

Mallory set the notebook aside and joined him at his laptop. She put the disc in, grinning when the screen went black followed by four weapons in a gold circle. A bow, dagger, staff and sword. They were replaced by gold writing. She read the words aloud. "Do you wish to return to Inadon?"

Before anyone could speak, there was a light knock on Ryan's bedroom door. They stared at it, Ryan finally crossing the room to unlock and open the door. "Mum."

Debra smiled, glancing past Ryan. "I didn't know everyone was here."

"Hi, Debra," Mallory said, her brother echoing her around his food, having started eating a packet of chips.

"Marty and I are going to the shops. Do either of you boys need anything?"

"We're good," Ryan said.

"We don't need anything. Thanks, Mum." Callum waited until his mum nodded and walked away and Ryan had closed and locked the door before he spoke. "Five minutes until two-thirty. We're leaving then.

Better make a note that my parents are going to the shops."

"I'm not going to have time to eat enough," Brodie protested.

"Eat faster," Ryan said.

"Don't tell him that. He will make himself sick." Mallory scribbled the information down then turned to her brother. "Put the food away. You'll have to wait until we're back to eat the rest of it." She left the notebook on the bed and returned to the laptop.

"That was my plan. But I haven't eaten enough." Brodie shoved a handful of chips in his mouth.

Callum got off the bed and slipped his feet into his sneakers, already wearing socks. "I've got coffee bags, instant coffee sachets and roasted coffee beans." He patted the pockets of his jeans. "I'm ready to go."

Ryan looked at each of them. "This time we need to focus on levelling up, improving our gear and earning money. We need to figure out how to teach Smudge to look after not only himself but also our gear when we're not there. We can't keep relying on people to look after everything. Who knows how trustworthy they'll be in other areas. We don't want to spend the rest of our time on Inadon living around Buckneth."

Mallory nodded. "I certainly want to see more of

Inadon." It was one of the things she loved about role-playing games. Exploring the world. She placed her hand on the mouse. "Everyone ready?"

"Not yet." Brodie shoved more chips in his mouth.

"Too bad," Mallory said. "We're going." Ignoring Brodie's protests, his mouthful now finished, she chose the 'yes' option.

Ryan drew her to him before the world went black, still holding onto her when smells, sounds and sensations returned. The darkness lightened to show they were in the same quiet corner of the tavern that they'd left from. There were a handful of patrons at some of the tables, who barely gave them a glance.

Callum checked his pockets. "None of it came with me. Not even the beans. There's got to be a way to get coffee to this world. How am I meant to start each day without it?"

Mallory couldn't resist smiling at the tone of desperation in Callum's voice. "I guess you'll have to find a different drink to have at breakfast."

"I can't believe you said that." Callum slowly shook his head. "A different drink."

"How about trying to bring coffee seeds and then you can plant them and always have coffee," Brodie said.

Callum checked his pockets one more time. "That

might work. I wonder where I'd get coffee seeds from." He sent Mallory a look. "A better idea than some have come up with."

"It'd be ages before you could harvest the beans," Ryan said.

"I might be able to find a mage who can make them grow quicker or a potion to speed up the growth," Callum said. "This is an RPG style world. Surely they have things like that."

Mallory checked that both layers of clothes had come with her. The t-shirt and the long sleeve one she wore over it. "Looks like we can bring layers of clothes. Next time we might be able to make some to bring with us and wear under our modern clothes so we can change out of the modern ones. We don't want to spend the money we earn in our world replacing clothes to keep our parents from wondering what happened to them."

"Let's get our gear and buy a fishing rod," Brodie said. "This time we need to do better with food. I'm not going hungry all the time." He led the way to the bar.

Ryan strode past him, reaching the bar first, waiting until Ahron finished talking to one of his customers before speaking. "We're ready to pick up our gear, Ahron. Thanks for looking after it for us."

Ahron nodded. "I thought you might be away longer. It hasn't been a day." He stepped out from behind the bar, beckoning the waitress over to take care of things. "This way."

They armed themselves and gathered their gear. Callum carried the basket of fruit and vegetables while Ryan took the backpack. Once they were organised, they bought some gear from Ahron. A fishing pole and a spare hook and line for seventeen copper pieces.

Mallory reluctantly counted out the money. So much for gaining money this time. She placed the coins on the bar, almost wincing when Ahron gathered them up. She managed not to voice her concerns.

"Could we hire your spyglass?" Ryan asked.

Mallory wanted to tell him no, that they couldn't afford it. But he was right. It would be useful. It was a pity they didn't have the gold to buy one of their own. They really needed to earn money. Like Ryan had said before they left, they needed to work on improving their gear. That was a bit hard to do without money.

"Hmm." Ahron looked at each of them. "One gold piece."

"Are you kidding?" Brodie demanded. "That's ridiculous."

For once Mallory agreed with her brother. "We can't afford that price."

"Eight silver pieces," Ahron said.

"That's still too much," Callum said.

"How about eight copper pieces?" Brodie asked. "We're only taking it with us while we're fishing. We'll bring it back in the morning. Not even a full day."

"Now you're the one being ridiculous," Ahron said. "I'd need at least four silver pieces."

"Four!" Brodie exclaimed. "Robbery. Nine copper pieces."

Chapter Three

Mallory stared at her brother. He was enjoying himself. It was something she'd never expected to see. Her brother haggling over prices.

"I should be the one crying robbery," Ahron said. "Two silver pieces and two of the fish you catch that are at least thirty-five centimetres in length."

"Two coins and two fish? I'd rather walk blind into a horde of goblins. Probably naked too. One silver piece and one fish," Brodie said.

"One silver piece and five fish."

Brodie laughed. "You're a comedian. One silver piece and four fish."

Ahron held out his hand. "Done."

For a moment Brodie looked startled, then he took Ahron's hand and shook it, a grin forming. He accepted the spyglass in its leather belt holster and handed it to Ryan before turning to Mallory for the money.

She winced at the amount of money they'd spent. They were down to five silver and five copper pieces. Not a good start. She turned away from the bar after saying goodbye to Ahron. "I wonder where we can sell fish."

Brodie grinned. "That was so much fun."

Ryan chuckled. "A comedian?" He undid his belt so he could slide the holster on.

Brodie laughed. "I thought that was inspired."

"Osbert senior is here." Callum nodded in the man's direction. "Think he'd let us collect Smudge before we go to the beach? We need to work on levelling his stats too if we want him to learn how to look after our gear for us. "

"Only one way to find out." Ryan led the way, stopping near Osbert. "Mind if we have a word?" He gave a nod to Osbert's companion before focusing his attention on the shepherd.

"If you want to know that your river otter is all right, there's nothing wrong with him," Osbert said. "Ninette spent all day pampering him and not getting her chores done. Useless girl. No better than her brothers."

"We were actually hoping it's not too late to collect

him this evening," Callum said. "We're going fishing and want to take him with us."

"You better not expect to claim Ninette needs to look after him for the unused hours of the day you paid. This is it. You collect him now and you have to pay again if you want her to take care of him," Osbert warned.

Callum nodded. "That's okay."

Osbert snorted. "You say that now." He finished off his drink, rising from the table. "Better make it quick then or she'll be off to bed. I won't have you waking her. It's hard enough getting her to help out around the farm without her being slowed down from lack of sleep."

Mallory tried not to smile at Osbert's steady stream of complaints. She was pretty certain that no matter what they said or did, he'd still find fault with it. The urge to smile faded and she felt a moment of sympathy for Ninette. No wonder the girl wanted to go off on adventures.

They followed Osbert outside, pausing by the door to light their lantern, Osbert carrying one of his own. Mallory glanced skywards. The moon was at least eighty percent visible so the village wasn't in complete darkness. She would have preferred something brighter than a lantern though. Like a modern spotlight. The shadows beside the buildings and under the trees could have contained anything. Like wolves or bandits. Or a rogue.

Reaching his farm, Osbert turned to face them. "Wait here." He ambled inside.

"Do you think we should be wandering around after dark?" Mallory scanned the area again. Had something moved by that tree? Or was it only her imagination.

"If we stay on the road we should be okay," Ryan said. "It's not completely dark. Between the moonlight and our lantern we should see anything that tries to attack."

"We need to find ways to earn a lot of money." Callum gave the basket to Brodie. "Fishing might be it."

"What–" Mallory was interrupted by Ninette coming outside, Smudge in her arms. He made soft chirruping noises, looking half asleep.

Callum gathered him up. "Did you miss me?" He laughed softly when Smudge chirruped again. "I'm going to take that as a yes. I missed you too." He rubbed Smudge's head.

"Where are you going?" Ninette asked. "Are you coming back?"

Callum shrugged. "We haven't figured out our plans yet."

Ninette stroked Smudge's head. "You will bring him back to visit me, won't you?"

"I should be able to do that before we leave the area. But I don't know how much longer we'll be staying around here." Callum glanced over his shoulder at his companions. "I need to go." With a smile, he took a step back. "Thanks for looking after him." He half turned away, nodding when Ninette raised her hand in farewell.

Mallory followed Callum back to the road, Ryan at her side, Brodie hurrying ahead to catch up with Callum. Again she felt a moment of sympathy for Ninette, wishing she could do something to help the girl, but they could barely help themselves. She scanned the area. "Are bears nocturnal?"

Ryan shrugged. "I wouldn't have a clue. Not that they will necessarily be like bears in our world."

Brodie looked over his shoulder. "Do you think the wagoner will give us enough time to visit Wayholt before we have to escort him to Surith?"

Ryan grinned. "If we offer to bring back more apples for his wife he might."

Brodie stumbled, needing to look forward. "Apple

pie sounds good. We should get a couple of pies made. They're good for breakfast."

"How would we store them?" Mallory asked. "They'd end up broken if we put them in the backpack."

"They could go in the basket," Brodie said. "With the fruit and veggies."

"I don't know." She eyed the basket he carried, not sure that was a much safer location. Especially not if he was carrying it.

Ryan chuckled. "I don't think they'd last long enough for the rest of us to get our share."

"As if I'd eat all of them," Brodie muttered.

Mallory looked towards Ryan, returning his grin. It looked like she wasn't the only one who doubted Brodie's willpower when it came to food. Especially delicious food. She remained silent, no one else speaking as they strode towards the beach. Their footsteps were loud in the night, not many sounds competing with them. There were a few rustles in the bushes and the call of animals in the distance, but nothing showed itself and about an hour later they reached the rocky shore. The sparse forest ended only metres from the beach, rocks and boulders scattered across the sand. A light breeze came from the direction of the ocean, bringing with it the scent of salt.

"That spot has a large enough patch of sand for us to set up camp." Brodie pointed to a location several metres from them.

"It should–" Mallory broke off when one of the 'rocks' near that location moved, claws waving about in front of it. A grin formed. "Giant mudcrabs." She was surprised by how excited she was to see them.

Ryan set the lantern on the sand and raised the spyglass to his eye, his shield in his other hand. "There are two of them. One a bit further away. They're called coastal mud crabs and have ten health points." He put the spyglass away, drawing his sword. "We'll take out the closest one first."

Callum set Smudge on the ground at his feet, readying his bow. "I guess they're nocturnal. Probably why we didn't see any the first day we arrived."

Brodie took out his throwing knives. "Are we attacking together? Because that thing is getting closer."

"Ready?" Ryan asked. When everyone nodded, or murmured an agreement, he said, "Attack."

Chapter Four

Mallory threw a fireball, barely causing the mud crab to halt, throwing another one when Brodie's knives and Callum's arrows bounced off the shell. "I don't know if I'm doing any damage." The initial joy at finding the crabs faded. What if they were too difficult for them to kill? The shell might make them invincible. She took a step back. Should they retreat?

The mud crab was close enough Ryan only needed to take two long steps towards it to attack with his sword. The mud crab rose up, attacking with its claws. Ryan managed to block the claws with his shield and strike the mud crab in the more vulnerable area underneath. Brodie and Callum attacked at the same time. They barely had time to register it was dead before the second crab was next to Ryan, rising up to attack him. Ryan struck it then jumped out of the way before the claws could reach him. Mallory,

Brodie and Callum attacked the vulnerable area underneath, while it was raised to attack. The mud crab collapsed on the sand.

Mallory grinned, glancing around the area, relief rushing through her. They hadn't been invincible after all. "A pity there aren't a few more. They're easy to kill. Once we could attack underneath them."

"I was expecting them to be tougher." Brodie collected his throwing knives. "Look at their shells. I reckon not much could get through them."

Ryan gestured towards the first mud crab. "Mallory and I will see what we can get out of this one while you two work on the other. Then we'll set up camp for the night and do some fishing." He grinned. "Someone is hoping to have fish for breakfast."

Smudge remained close to Callum, chirruping now the danger was over. He followed Callum to the mud crab, taking some of the meat they managed to harvest. They also got a claw while Ryan and Mallory gained one claw and a shell.

Ryan examined the shell. "We're going to need a packhorse at some stage. Especially if we get a lot of bulky drops like this."

"Do you want to set up camp in the spot I found?" Brodie asked.

"Should be a good location." Ryan strode towards

the spot, dropping his backpack down, putting the shell next to it. "Mallory and I will gather firewood, Callum can start to fish and Brodie can be on guard duty. Try using some of that crab meat for bait."

Mallory picked up the lantern, keeping hold of her wand. "There's a larger clump of trees over there." She nodded in the direction further along the beach.

"I might leave this behind." Ryan started to put his shield near the backpack.

"It's night. Anything could be around here. Take it with you." Callum stood at the water's edge, his line in the water. Smudge sat beside him, leaning against his leg, making soft noises.

Ryan nodded. "Once you catch a fish, it's Brodie's turn. We should all unlock fishing. Who knows how useful it might end up being." He started towards the clump of trees, glancing at Mallory. "You coming?"

Catching up with him, she strode beside him. "I wonder how much money we'll get for the claws and shell. It'd be nice if we could earn back some of the money we spent tonight."

Ryan started to speak, raising his shield at the sound of a roar as they entered the trees. The creature landed on the shield, knocking it from Ryan's hands and landing on the ground in front of them.

Mallory froze for a second at the sight of the

frenzied creature. "It's a drop bear." The words burst from her as the large grey animal, with tufted ears, picked himself up off the ground. Shaking, he snarled, showing a mouth full of sharp teeth and long incisors. Heart racing, she threw a fireball at him as he lumbered towards her, the lantern light splashing around crazily as she stumbled backwards.

Ryan attacked with his sword. The creature snarled, swiping at him with sharp claws. Ryan got in a second attack before he was forced to retreat.

Mallory threw another fireball at the drop bear, stumbling as she backed away when the creature turned towards her. She threw a third fireball. It missed, the creature having launched itself forward. Heart racing, breath coming fast, she threw another fireball as she tried to retreat, running into a tree. The drop bear snarled again before collapsing on the ground, unmoving. She stared at the still body before glancing at the clump of trees in front of her. "Think there are more in there?" She was tempted to retreat further.

Ryan sheathed his sword and crouched by the large creature. "I don't know. But we might want to stay out of large clumps of trees. We should find enough wood lying around the edges." He took out his skinning knife. "Want to give me a hand?"

She tucked the wand into the canvas loop she'd made for it and took out her dagger, setting the lantern on the ground next to them. "We should have waited until morning. We can hardly see anything." She scanned the area. Nothing seemed to move.

"It would have taken too many days in our world."

"We could have hung out in the tavern." She helped him try to skin the creature.

Ryan chuckled. "Brodie would have been hassling you to spend coins on alcohol."

A smile reluctantly formed. "I suppose." Her smile faded when they didn't manage to get a pelt. They only ended up with four claws.

"I wonder if they're used for alchemy. They don't look big enough to be used for weapons. Not like bear claws." Ryan slipped the claws into a pocket. "We'll grab some wood and get a fire started."

"I can't believe there are drop bears here. It looked exactly like I thought one would. An overgrown, rabid koala." Sheathing her dagger, she left the lantern on the ground as she gathered firewood. Quickly finding an armful, she picked up the lantern, her gaze continually scanning the area as she listened for any approaching creatures.

Ryan filled his arms with firewood before he collected the shield the drop bear had knocked from his hands. "Lucky I brought my shield with me. I might have lost a lot of health otherwise."

As they headed back to camp, she couldn't resist checking his journal page to make sure he was okay. He had nineteen of his twenty-one health. She flicked to her main journal page, checking her stats as they returned to camp. "I've got eighty-two XP. Not long and I'll gain another CAS point. Then I'll be another point closer to levelling up my character and gaining access to the warrior class." She needed something better than a dagger for close combat. Especially if they were going to keep running into creatures like bears, wolves and drop bears. Why did so many of the creatures on Inadon have fangs? Even mountain rabbits had them.

"I might put another point in hunting when I gain one." Ryan dumped the firewood near the blanket Smudge was now curled up on. He raised his head and chirruped at the noise.

Mallory smiled, washing the blood from her hands in the ocean before helping Ryan start a campfire, lighting it with the help of the lantern. She glanced over her shoulder. "Have you caught anything yet, Callum?"

"Not yet. I had to take a break and make sure Smudge was comfortable. Poor thing was tired."

Once the fire was built up, Mallory sat on the second blanket with Ryan, leaning against him as she told Brodie and Callum about the fight.

Brodie looked off into the darkness. "Think there are more? I want to see a drop bear."

Mallory shuddered, glancing towards the trees in the distance, little more than shadowy shapes. "I miss modern lighting."

"I've got a fish." Callum removed the hook from the struggling fish. It had see-through gold coloured fins and tail. "You have unlocked fishing, a crafting ability that allows you to catch, clean and prepare fish using various methods."

Ryan checked the fish through the spyglass. "It's called a gold fin." He put the spyglass away. "We really need one of these."

"We need a lot of things," Brodie said.

"We also need to gain a character level," Mallory said.

"It's my turn." Brodie took the fishing pole off Callum and cast the line out once he'd added crabmeat for bait.

Ryan eyed the fish. "This one doesn't look big enough to pay Ahron."

"What if we don't get any that are big enough."

She looked at the fish. "What if that's as big as they get?"

Ryan shrugged. "We'll sort something out. Maybe give Ahron extra fish."

She took a deep breath, trying not to think of all the problems facing them. How were they meant to level up, gain better gear and earn money? In an effort not to think about how little progress they were making she tried to focus on their surroundings. "It's nice on the beach with a campfire."

Ryan chuckled. "Unless a mud crab comes along and ruins the atmosphere."

Chapter Five

A smile formed, fading as Mallory's worries crowded back in. "I wouldn't mind. I need a bit more XP." She was so close to her next CAS point. Levelling up, lack of gear and limited funds pressed in on her. "I want to go to other areas, but I'm worried we're too low a level to go far from where we started."

He slung an arm around her shoulders, drawing her close. "That makes sense." He paused a moment. "We can gather herbs in the morning if we don't level up while fishing."

She nearly sighed. Surely there was a better way than that to level up. "We're not going to fish all night, are we?" Mallory asked.

"No. Probably take turns sleeping, fishing and guarding. Two can sleep each time," Ryan said. "That way we should get our sleeping pattern back to normal. No point wasting daylight when it costs us to use the lantern." He leaned forward and picked up the lantern, putting it out. He set it down beside the blanket, draping his arm around her shoulders again. "We'll make do with the campfire. We don't have a lot of oil."

This time a sigh did escape. "We need to find a good source of income. Having to watch every coin we spend is tedious."

Ryan tightened his arm around her. "We'll get there eventually. Once we gain a few levels we'll start earning more money and gaining XP quicker. Look at most RPGs. The low levels are always a struggle. And if Jed is right, and they've been based on Inadon, then we'll eventually earn more money and gain better drops as we level up."

She stared into the flickering flames of the campfire, slipping her arm around his waist. Some of her worries eased. How many role-playing games had she played? She should know by now that the beginning was usually slow going when it came to earning experience points, money and gear. Another smile formed, this one remaining. And yet each time she became impatient with her progress and wanted to rush through those early levels. She needed to learn to enjoy them. Especially here. This was after all a dream come true. "Sitting on the beach by a campfire is better than going to see a movie."

He laughed softly. "Yeah. It certainly is. We're still going to do something together. Just you and me." He glanced towards Callum and Brodie. "Without our brothers."

She laughed softly, continuing to stare into the flames. She didn't recall falling asleep. But somehow she ended curled up next to Ryan, his arm around her waist, his body curved around her back. Blinking several times, she tried to focus on who was shaking her shoulder.

"Time for you two to keep watch and fish." Callum shook her shoulder again before shaking Ryan's.

She tried to stretch, the movement difficult with Ryan's arm across her. "What time is it?"

"I don't know. But you must have been asleep for a few hours," Callum said. "Or at least long enough for Brodie to eat two apples."

Mallory laughed, starting to draw away from Ryan. "That doesn't mean much with how often Brodie eats."

"We've slept for at least two hours because my health is full." Ryan drew her back, giving her a brief kiss before letting go and looking up at his brother. "Did you catch many fish?"

Callum stood up. "Five. We've got enough for Ahron. One of them must be half a metre in length."

Mallory stood, stretching and yawning. "How are we going to carry all of them back to Buckneth?"

"We put the fruit and veggies in the backpack. The fish are in the basket," Callum said.

Brodie looked up from where he sat at the water's edge, holding the fishing pole. "Who's taking over?"

"I can." Ryan strode towards him, taking the pole and remaining standing.

Mallory added more wood to the campfire, which was starting to die down, while Brodie stretched out on the blanket she and Ryan had vacated and Callum curled up next to Smudge on the other one. She smiled when Smudge made soft sounds, snuggling closer to Callum. The river otter was certainly cute and she didn't blame Callum for wanting to buy him even though they were running low on money. Finished stoking up the fire she moved closer to Ryan.

He draped an arm around her shoulders. "Not sure if I should be concerned that our first date is going fishing. Not exactly what I expected."

"This isn't a date. And if it was, we wouldn't be fishing."

"Really? What would we be doing?"

She laughed at the tone of voice he used. The words she started to say forgotten when there was a tug on the line and he worked on reeling in a fish. She took a step back when she was sprayed with saltwater. "I guess it's my turn next." As he unhooked the fish, she looked it over. "I wonder if gold fins are the only ones in this area." Taking the pole, she baited the hook and cast the line into the water. "That one doesn't look big enough for Ahron."

Ryan put the fish in the basket, laying it on top of the other ones. Fish hung over both ends of the basket. "Probably only thirty centimetres in length, give or take a few centimetres." He returned to her side, after washing his hands in the sea, this time sliding his arm around her waist.

"There are so many things we need to buy. Maybe there's a reason why they expect you to be at least eighteen to travel to Inadon. How are we meant to survive?" Her worries rushed back in on her.

"In some ways, we were probably better off not reading the welcome pack they sent. I've got all the rules and information in my head and I keep worrying about not passing the test to become a guardian." He turned slightly so he was facing her. "How about we forget everything except enjoying ourselves and go back to marvelling about being in an RPG?"

She slowly nodded, her body relaxing. It was basically what she'd been trying to convince herself of earlier. "It is like a dream come true." She felt a tug on the fishing line. "I've got something already."

"Don't wind it in too quickly. The line might snap."

"How do you know?"

"Dad took me fishing a couple of times when I was younger. Before we decided it was going to take more than a couple of fishing trips to find common ground. I guess he decided not to put Callum through the same trauma since he never invited him to go fishing."

She slowly brought the fish in, letting the line loosen a couple of times when the pole bent dramatically. "I think it's the same size as yours." She struggled to remove the hook. "Can't it stay still?"

Ryan chuckled. "Don't you think you'd struggle too?"

She put it in the basket with the rest of them, about to check her journal, the icon in the top left hand corner of her vision, when Smudge sat up making repetitive high-pitched chirping sounds. She recognised the noise instantly, dropping the fishing pole to reach for her wand and dagger.

Ryan drew his sword. "Over there." He pointed to three bandits, one drawing back an arrow.

Brodie and Callum scrambled to their feet, reaching for weapons.

Mallory threw a fireball at the archer bandit, causing him to drop his arrow. The other two bandits ran towards them, wielding short swords. She threw a second fireball at the archer, not sure if she should attack the two who were closing in on Ryan. Before she needed to make a decision, Callum shot the archer with an arrow and Brodie tossed two throwing knives at him. He dropped to the ground and she attacked one of the bandits going after Ryan.

"Couldn't they have waited until I had a sleep?" Brodie threw a knife at each bandit. "It's not like it's easy to fall asleep when your body isn't used to a time zone."

Callum also shot each bandit and Ryan attacked first one and then the other before he needed to retreat. Mallory launched a fireball at the second bandit, since he was closest to Ryan. Another fireball and he collapsed on the ground, the last bandit taken down by a throwing knife.

Brodie victory punched the air. "Did you see that? Now that's what happens when you wake me."

Chapter Six

Mallory chuckled, slowly shaking her head at her brother's antics. "Unless it's to offer you food." She scanned the area, finding no other bandits, surprised the fight had finished so quickly.

"Of course," Brodie said. "Food makes everything better."

"No, that's coffee. It makes everything better." Callum collected his arrows.

"No, food. You wouldn't survive without it." Brodie gathered his throwing knives.

Callum patted Smudge, telling him how good he was. "I don't think we need to stand guard of a night. Smudge is a brilliant guard." He offered the river otter a piece of crabmeat.

Smudge yipped a couple of times then grunted, taking the crabmeat and immediately beginning to eat.

"I wonder if that's a yes," Mallory said.

"If someone wants to search the bandits, I'll take the bodies further away from our camp in case they draw in wild animals," Ryan said. "We all need some sleep tonight, even if we're not tired. We're walking to Wayholt tomorrow. If the wagoner can wait to go to Surith."

"It probably already is tomorrow." Callum strode to one of the bandits.

Mallory glanced at Ryan. "You're not moving them away from the camp on your own." She searched a bandit while Brodie searched the third one. Between them, they found a short bow, two arrows, five copper pieces and a tunic that looked like it hadn't been washed in months. She held it out, making a face when the smell of it drifted towards her. "Do we really want to keep this?"

Ryan took it from her, tossing it to the side. "I'll wash it in the sea once I've dumped the bodies." He turned to Callum and Brodie. "You pair stay awake. Fish or something while we're gone. But make sure you keep an eye out. This place isn't exactly safe between mud crabs, drop bears and bandits."

Mallory lit the lantern, using a twig she held in the campfire, and followed Ryan who carried a bandit over his shoulder. They were about ten metres from their camp, when she said, "I keep forgetting to take my long sleeve shirt off. I need something to wear home so Mum doesn't ask questions I can't answer."

Ryan held out his hand, having left his shield at the camp. "I can carry the lantern if you want to go back and put your shirt in the backpack." He grinned. "I'm sure your mum would find a way to blame it on me if you returned home with your shirt torn and bloody."

"I don't want to think about the reason she'd come up with. It's not like we could explain the truth to her. At least not without adding her to our party and bringing her here. Then she'd try and confiscate the disc so we could never return." Mallory handed over the lantern. "I won't be long." She started to unbutton her long sleeve shirt before she turned away.

"Wait up." Ryan put the lantern and bandit on the sand near a large rock. "I better do the same. Mum and Dad won't have left when we get back. Just in case she thinks of something else to ask, and I don't have time to change, I better not arrive back in tatters." He took off his long sleeve shirt, dropping it on the sand by his feet before pulling his t-shirt over his head.

Mallory watched him, a smile half forming when he chuckled. "What can you expect? It wasn't like you told me to turn my back."

He pulled on his long sleeve shirt, leaving it unbuttoned as he stepped close. "Are you coming back after you put our shirts in the backpack?" When she nodded he kissed her, giving her the shirt as he stepped away.

She remained where she was for a moment, watching him button his shirt before he collected the bandit and lantern. Turning, she ran back to the camp, enough moonlight that she was able to avoid the many boulders and rocks scattered across the beach. She put both their shirts in the backpack, remembering to check her journal as she did so. The icon that had remained in the corner of her vision had been a notification about her new skill like she'd expected. *You have unlocked fishing, a crafting ability that allows you to catch, clean and prepare fish using various methods.*

"What's going on?" Brodie asked.

"We didn't take off our spare shirts for when we go home." Mallory stood up, stepping away from the backpack. "Mum won't forget what we were wearing when we left."

Brodie handed the fishing pole to Callum. "I forgot about that too." He unbuttoned his long sleeve shirt.

"I'll be back soon." Mallory ran along the beach, again managing to avoid the many rocks scattered in front of her. She caught up with Ryan and took the lantern from him. "How far are we going?"

Ryan half shrugged. "Five minutes or so should do it." He glanced over his shoulder. "Everything okay at the camp?"

"They're fishing again."

"We should probably make a hollow in the sand and bake one or two of the fish in there. Gut it and cover it with sand and build a fire over it."

"That sounds okay. Will it work?" A whistling noise ahead of them drew her attention. She peered along the beach. There were too many shadows for her to figure out what was making the sound.

"Should do. Other food can be cooked like that." He paused a moment. "Did you want to wait here while I go ahead and see what that noise is?"

"Yeah, right. I'm not about to let you walk into trouble on your own." She eyed the tumble of boulders the noise seemed to be coming from. "Should you leave the bandit here while we have a closer look?"

"I'll dump him over near the side of the boulders and then we can go around the front for a better look." Ryan took the lead.

Mallory slid her wand out of the canvas loop she'd put it back into, holding the lantern up in the hope the light would go further. "Should we wait until morning?"

Ryan dumped the bandit at the side of the boulder, drawing his sword before he headed towards the water.

This close, Mallory realised there was solid rock behind the tumble of boulders. The whistling sound increased as they moved around to the front and found the entrance to a cave. She peered inside, an icon appearing in the corner of her vision. Seeing there was nothing inside, only the remains of a campfire, she checked her journal, reading out the notification. "You have gained fifteen experience points for discovering Bard's Hollow." She grinned. "Yes. I've gained another CAS point." Not that she knew what to put it into.

"I've gained one too. I'm definitely going to put mine into hunting. I really need to level it up more." Ryan took another step into the cave. "There's a tunnel at the back. It slopes down."

She wanted to grab hold of him and tug him out of the cave, but her hands were full. "Come back. We don't know what's in there." The eerie whistling sound the wind made entering the cave was enough to mask softer sounds. Like someone sneaking up the tunnel towards them. "We've got other plans for today." At least she guessed Callum was right and it was now their fourth day. It had to be well past midnight by now. "We need to dump the rest of the bodies. Brodie and Callum should probably take turns coming here with you." She grinned. "Or Brodie will be complaining about missing out on the XP."

Ryan chuckled, stepping out of the cave. "We'll put it to the vote when everyone else has seen it."

"We came back to do the quest the guardians set us." She walked at his side, glancing around the area as they headed towards the campsite.

"I wonder if they'd complain if we were distracted by side quests instead of doing that one."

"It might mean they'd fail us." She'd have to ask one of the guardians when they returned home. There was so much they didn't know.

Chapter Seven

Mallory and Ryan remained silent for the rest of the walk back to their camp, finding Brodie trying to put another fish in the basket. He stood staring at the basket, the fish he'd added draped over the handle. "We're going to have to eat some of them. There's no way we can get all of them back to Buckneth."

Smudge bounded over to Brodie, making excited squeaks as he stood on his hind legs, one paw on Brodie's leg, the other held out.

Mallory laughed. "I think he agrees."

"You've got another CAS point," Callum said.

"What?" Brodie frowned. "You have. You're miles ahead of me. I've only got eighty-five XP."

"We found a cave." Ryan hoisted the next bandit onto his shoulder. "If you want to carry the lantern you can come with me."

Brodie took the lantern from Mallory, looking over

his shoulder at Callum as he followed Ryan. "Try not to catch anything until I come back to take over. Everyone is ahead of me." He stumbled on a rock, the lantern scattering light randomly across the beach.

Mallory winced. "I hope he doesn't break that lantern. We can't afford another one."

Callum nodded towards the fishing pole. "You want to look after this while I give Smudge something to eat?"

Mallory smiled at Smudge, who remained by the basket of fish. "Yeah. He looks very cute with that pleading expression." Taking the fishing pole from Callum, she sat on the sand, staring out to sea. Moonlight spread across the waves, rippling and shimmering with the movement of the water. It was surprisingly relaxing sitting on the beach fishing considering they'd not long fought three bandits.

The moment Brodie returned, he took over fishing. "Did you catch any?"

Mallory shook her head. "You should get some sleep."

"As if I can sleep now. We should explore that cave. I need one more XP so I can get a CAS point."

Mallory started to list the reasons why exploring Bard's Hollow wasn't a good idea, but decided to wait until everyone was back so she didn't have to repeat herself. The moment Ryan and Callum returned from getting rid of the last body, Brodie repeated his earlier statement about exploring the cave.

Callum sat on the blanket beside Smudge, absently patting him. "We're coming back to this area after we escort the wagoner to Surith."

"We should see what's in the cave now," Brodie said. "It's not like we have to wait for day or anything. Caves are dark so it doesn't matter what time we explore it."

Before Mallory could comment, Callum spoke. "We don't know how big it is. It could take us days to explore. We've got that quest from the guardians and you want to see the girl in Wayholt."

"We don't have to do the quest," Brodie said.

"We might have to if we want to join the guardians," Ryan said. "They did send it to us."

Brodie looked at each of them. "What if we go a little way in?"

Ryan raised his hand. "Hands up who wants to wait."

Mallory raised a hand, grinning when Callum did the same. She turned to her brother. "I guess we explore the cave another day."

Callum gave Smudge a piece of crabmeat. "We

should try and sleep, Brodie. It's a long walk to Wayholt."

"As if I c–" He broke off when the end of his fishing pole bent towards the water. "I've got another one." After reeling it in, he stood holding it. "What am I going to do with it? No more will fit in the basket."

Ryan took the fish from Brodie. "I'll cook this one and the last one you caught so we can have them for breakfast."

Brodie's expression brightened. "We can eat the fish? We don't have to live off berries."

Mallory grinned at her brother's expression. "Didn't you tell us we have to do better with food this time?"

Brodie victory punched the air. "Hell yeah!" He returned to the water's edge and cast the line out. "There's definitely no way I can sleep now. How long will it take to cook?"

Ryan shrugged in answer.

"Well, I'm getting some sleep." Callum stretched out beside Smudge who snuggled up close, making soft sounds.

By the time Mallory had helped Ryan prepare the fish, gathered more firewood from some trees nearby and the fish had finished cooking, Brodie had caught another two fish and the sun was rising. He'd also gained his CAS point. While she boiled finely diced potatoes in a pot of saltwater, Brodie woke Callum. They had to share the two wooden bowls, Brodie watching that Callum didn't take any of the food from his half of the bowl.

"This is more like what I expected." Ryan gestured towards the campfire that was nearly out and the food they were eating. "I could get used to this." He grinned. "Once we learn to cook a little better."

"Are we going to look for somewhere near the ocean when we search for a good place for a base?" Mallory took a piece of fish from the bowl she shared with Ryan. He was right. They did need to improve their cooking skills. But the meal wasn't too bad. It was a lot better than berries.

"We should look for somewhere with lots of resources," Callum said.

"I guess it'll depend on what we need," Ryan said. "No point having heaps of resources in the area if they're not the resources we need."

"We should set up on the mainland," Brodie said. "There'll be more places to explore over there. It's not like islands are very big."

"Australia is an island." Callum finished off his share of the food.

"That's different." Brodie took the empty bowl to the ocean to wash it.

It didn't take long to clean up after their meal and Brodie suggested going for a swim before they headed to Buckneth. Mallory looked at her clothes then at the boys stripping down to their boxers. She sighed. "I don't have anything to wear."

"I washed that tunic we got earlier," Ryan said. "It's big enough it'll probably reach your knees." He pointed to a boulder where an army green tunic was spread out to dry. "It's only a little damp. Not that being damp will matter if you want to go for a swim."

She looked from the tunic to the ocean where Callum, Brodie and Smudge were enjoying themselves. "Okay. I'll get changed behind that boulder over there." She pointed to a larger one about eight metres away.

"Want me to keep guard for you?" Ryan grinned.

Rolling her eyes, she grabbed the tunic and headed for the boulder. A glance around showed it was more sheltered than she'd thought with another smaller boulder on the other side. It didn't take her long to change into the tunic, which reached mid-thigh, and she returned to the campsite, leaving her gear by the fire. She kept hold of her wand. "Should we leave all our weapons behind?" She thought of the bandits who'd tried to sneak up on them earlier.

Smudge burst out of the water, holding a fish that struggled to escape. He tried to give it to Callum who nearly lost it. Smudge chattered at Callum.

Brodie laughed. "I think he's saying you're clumsy."

Callum took the fish to the shore, draping it over the basket. "Like you can talk. King of dexterity fails." He grinned when Brodie answered him with a single raised finger.

Mallory put her wand with the rest of her gear, not sure how the timber weapon would fare in the ocean. She took her dagger from its sheath, walking towards the water with it. She wouldn't feel safe without some kind of weapon. Not after the creatures they'd encountered in the area.

Callum collected his hunting knife. "You're probably right. Bard's Hollow isn't far away and there might be anything in the water."

Brodie scanned the waves. "Why did you have to go and say that? Now how am I meant to enjoy myself?"

Callum strode into the water. "Smudge can keep an eye out for danger. He seems to be good at it."

He patted Smudge when the otter swam around him several times, diving away after a moment.

Chapter Eight

Mallory walked out far enough in the water so she could sink beneath the waves. Several metres away she saw a fish darting through the water, obviously heading for somewhere less crowded and quieter. Smiling, she started to surface. Movement further out to sea caught her attention. Needing air, she surfaced. "There are mermaids out there. Riding some kind of fish horse."

"Were they kelpies?" Callum sank beneath the waves.

Mallory shrugged, going beneath the surface again, noticing the rest of her companions did the same. Behind the mermaids, who rode creatures that looked to be half horse and half fish, was another figure that glanced in their direction.

The creature stopped following the mermaids, who continued riding north. It turned towards them. The narrow, sleek body had a green cast to it, legs kept together as it propelled itself forward with a dolphin like movement. Smudge came arrowing towards them from deeper waters, something clutched in his paw, nudging them towards the shore.

Mallory rose for a breath, sinking beneath the water again. The creature had come close enough she could see the sleek body was female. The body of the creature was either clad in a fitted outfit of scales or covered in scales from chest to thighs. Her long hair streamed behind her and when she opened her mouth, it was to reveal sharp, pointed, shark-like teeth.

Again Mallory rose from the water, the creature doing the same. Smudge made his repetitive high-pitched chirping sounds that signalled danger and she backed away from the creature.

Ryan grabbed her arm. "Hurry. If we're lucky she won't be able to come onto the land."

"I wouldn't count on it. She has legs." Callum ran through the water, frequently glancing over his shoulder.

Mallory splashed towards the shore, continuing to clutch the dagger, glancing over her shoulder as frequently as her companions. "What is it?"

The creature remained in the deeper water, close

enough Mallory could see the webbed fingers the creature held out to them, beckoning them to the depths. She began to sing. The melodic voice drifted across the waves, the song enticing.

Mallory slowed her steps, Ryan doing the same.

"She's so beautiful." Brodie faced the creature, taking a step towards her.

Smudge launched himself first at Brodie and then at Callum. Both fell backwards into the water, spluttering as they rose. Mallory and Ryan took several steps towards the creature, Mallory looking between the shore and out to sea, unable to think of anything other than answering the call.

Callum raced to the shore. "It's an undine." He grabbed up his bow and an arrow, spinning to fire at the creature who stopped mid-song, screeching as she sank beneath the waves.

Mallory froze, shaking her head, trying to clear the enticing song from her mind. "She…" She shook her head again.

Ryan clasped her hand. "I could only think of joining her."

Smudge swam around them, pushing them towards the shore.

Ryan bent and patted Smudge's head. "I hear you. Time to get out of the water."

Mallory clung to Ryan's hand as they splashed through the water to the shore, his grip equally tight. "I wasn't thinking. I automatically walked towards her." She shuddered as she thought of the sharp teeth. "Would we have fought her while she sang?"

Callum was pulling his clothes on over wet limbs. "I doubt it." He gathered his weapons. "I thought they only enticed those interested in females. But I couldn't resist her either."

Ryan began to pull on his clothes. "I guess not."

Mallory gathered up her gear. "Their song must work on everyone. Or at least humans." She smiled down at Smudge who still clutched something in his hand. "It doesn't work on river otters."

Smudge yipped a couple of times, tossing the object into the air and catching it.

Mallory had started to turn away, planning on going behind the boulder to get changed. She stared open-mouthed at the item Smudge played with. "That's a pearl."

Callum crouched in front of Smudge, holding out his hand for the object. "It is. A hole has been drilled through it. I wonder if the rest of the pearl necklace is out there." He handed it back to Smudge.

"What are you doing?" Brodie demanded. "We could sell it and get better gear."

"Smudge found it." Callum rose to his feet. "It's up to him if he wants to sell it. And if we do, it should be to get something for him. Not us."

"He's your pet," Brodie argued.

"He's my companion animal," Callum said.

Mallory left them to their discussion, heading behind the boulder. Once she was dressed and fully armed she rejoined her party, noticing that everything was packed and there were two canvas wrapped bundles next to the basket, the crab shell and claws tied atop the blankets on the backpack. She used some of the water from the waterskin to rinse off the dagger she'd taken into the ocean, not sure what the saltwater would do to the metal if it wasn't cleaned.

"How are we meant to cart ten fish all the way to Buckneth?" Brodie demanded. "We should have eaten more of them."

Smudged yipped a couple of times, standing next to Callum and playing with his pearl.

"He needs his own little bag to carry his things in," Mallory said.

"That's a good idea." Callum looked down at Smudge. "What do you reckon?" Callum smiled when Smudge yipped again.

"Don't encourage him," Brodie muttered.

Mallory laughed. "Are we ready to go?"

Ryan picked up the backpack and grabbed the basket, fishing pole and his shield once the backpack was in place. "We should go. That undine might decide to come back."

Callum and Brodie both picked up a canvas parcel of fish, Brodie muttering about not having eaten enough of them. Mallory walked beside Ryan, scanning the area, her right hand close to her dagger and the wet tunic in her left hand.

By the time they arrived in the village, the tunic was partially dry and Mallory was carrying one of the parcels of fish. Smudge had only bounded along at Callum's side for half the journey, regularly stopping to check various plants and objects along the side of the road. They'd passed several plants along the way that could be harvested, but none of them could carry anything else with their arms filled with fish or in Callum's case, Smudge.

"Probably a good thing we didn't explore that cave," Ryan said. "It's enough of an effort to get this stuff back."

As they approached the door of the tavern, Mallory looked over her shoulder to Callum. "How did you know it was an undine?"

"I did some research on mythical creatures and read up on medieval life while we were home."

"Why didn't you tell the rest of us?" Brodie asked.

"I tried to tell you, but you kept telling me to be quiet while you did your homework," Callum said.

Ryan grinned. "I'm pretty sure I heard Brodie say that a few times this week." He pushed the tavern door open, holding it until everyone was inside.

"I don't want to get grounded," Brodie muttered. "Or banned from playing games."

"You're back nice and early," Ahron said. "My spyglass is undamaged?"

Ryan set the basket on the floor along with his shield and the fishing pole before he handed over the spyglass. "Thanks." He took the fish from Brodie, unwrapping the canvas. "Are these suitable?"

"Perfect." Ahron took the fish. "Let me put them in the kitchen."

Chapter Nine

Mallory waited until Ahron was out of sight before she spoke. "What are we meant to do with six fish? Can we eat them before they go off?"

The door opened and the wagoner stepped in as Ryan spoke. "We might be able to sell them in Wayholt."

"I don't suppose you're interested in going in the other direction." The wagoner joined them at the bar.

"We were going to talk to you about you needing an escort to Surith and back," Mallory said.

"How soon do you need to go?" Ryan asked.

"We wanted to go to Wayholt first," Brodie said. "There's someone I want to see and a quest at South Peak Mine we want to do."

"You're coming back this way afterwards?" the wagoner asked.

"We can escort you to Surith when we return," Callum said.

"How do you feel about escorting me the fifteen kilometres to Wayholt and then the twenty-five kilometres to South Peak Mine the next day? I haven't had the opportunity to go to Wayholt for a while and it would be good to buy ores from the mine to trade at Surith. I can help you sell your fish in Wayholt, and whatever else you might want sold, without charging my usual fee," the wagoner said. "I can set aside a chest on the wagon for your use during the journey and pay you a silver piece if we return safely to Buckneth."

"When would you want to leave?" Ryan asked.

The wagoner took out a pocket watch. "I can be ready in two hours. So a quarter to eleven." He put the pocket watch away. "That won't be too late for you?"

Brodie turned to Mallory. "We could pick herbs to sell to the apothecary."

Mallory nodded. "Can we put things in the chest now?" She really didn't want to lug around their extra gear while they were gathering herbs.

"If you give me a hand to put the chests on the wagon," the wagoner said.

"You've got a deal," Ryan said. "We can escort

you to Wayholt today and on to South Peak Mine tomorrow and we'll discuss the trip to Surith when we return to Buckneth."

The wagoner held out his hand. "Sounds good to me."

They each shook his hand, saying goodbye to Ahron who returned to the bar as they were leaving. The wagon was behind the wagoner's home and the chests were lined up along the back of the building, a canvas covering each of them. They helped put six large chests on the wagon, three along each side with space down the middle where the wagoner told them they could ride. After they placed the fish, crab shell and crab claws in the chest the wagoner said they could use, and left the shield and fishing pole in the wagon, they headed off to collect herbs. They also grabbed two baskets from the baker to collect berries so they'd have pie after they returned from Wayholt.

While they picked berries, Mallory read out the update to their quest. "Trade Route Guard: The wagoner has postponed his journey to Surith, but is interested in an escort there and back when he returns from Wayholt." Mallory looked at the new quest, reading it aloud too. "Trading Opportunity: For safe escort to Wayholt and South Peak Mine the wagoner is willing to trade up to one chest worth of goods on your behalf and pay you a silver piece upon safe return to Buckneth."

"A silver piece sounds good," Callum said. "Especially since we were going there and back anyway."

"Yeah," Brodie agreed. "Like being paid for something you planned to do. And being able to ride in his wagon will be good. Twenty-five kilometres is a long way to walk."

"Only about five to six hours, depending on your pace," Ryan said.

Mallory interrupted her brother's complaints about walking so far. "I wonder if the wagoner will get a better price than we did for our herbs." She dropped another handful of berries into the basket at her feet.

Once they'd given the baskets of berries to the baker and said they'd like their pie in three days, they visited Ninette so she could say goodbye to Smudge.

"Are you coming back here?" Ninette cuddled Smudge, the river otter making chirruping sounds.

Callum nodded. "We'll be back in three days."

"I wish I could go with you." Ninette handed Smudge to Callum. "But I need to stay and help Pa. There's no way I could afford the gear I'd need to travel around like Great-Great-Grandma did. Not with how little Pa pays me."

"You might be able to if you didn't spend your money on river otters and kittens," Brodie said.

Ninette's eyes narrowed. "Two gold pieces every six months isn't enough to outfit anyone. And he only started paying me that last year when I turned fifteen."

Mallory stepped slightly in front of her brother, surprised the girl was a year older than she'd thought. She doubted Brodie's charisma level would help with the look Ninette was giving him. "We better go. We have herbs to pick before we leave."

Ninette stood by the farmhouse, waving to them.

"I feel bad about her being stuck there," Callum spoke softly. "Especially since she spent half her money on Smudge and I bet Osbert didn't give her any of the money we gave him."

"It's not like we've got spare money to give her," Brodie said.

Callum glanced over his shoulder. "We might one day though."

Mallory nodded. She liked Callum's idea. One day they'd have money to spend and they could help her then.

Reaching Buckneth, they washed the scent of fish from the basket before gathering herbs, the faint glimmer to resources making it easy to find them once they were close. They filled the basket with a mixture of meadowsweet and calendula, adding some to the backpack when it was full. They didn't range too far from the village, wanting to avoid getting caught up in any battles and be late to meet the wagoner.

When they returned, he was saying goodbye to his wife, the wagon out the front of his home, two dapple grey highland ponies hooked up to his wagon. Once the herbs were in the chest, and Mallory had suggested they use the outhouse since there was no way she was going behind a tree, along the way where a creature could disturb her, they spread out the blankets in the middle of the wagon and clambered up.

Mallory sat at the end, her legs hanging over the edge of the wagon. Ryan sat beside her, the other two stretched out to take a nap with Smudge who was curled up between them, having finished off the last of the crabmeat. He still clutched his pearl in his paw. As the wagon moved forward, Mallory checked her stats, trying to decide what to do with her CAS point. She smiled as she looked at her experience points. She had fifteen, as they all did. Brodie had insisted on keeping things even. As always.

"What are you doing?" Ryan draped his arm around her shoulders, drawing her close.

"Trying to decide what to do with my available CAS point." She kept her voice low, not wanting to wake Brodie and Callum.

"I forgot about that." Ryan paused for a moment. "You have reached level two hunting. You are ten percent more likely to gain meat from wild animals you have hunted and harvested."

"That sounds good. I'm just not sure what to put mine into. Cooking or alchemy. I want to do more with my alchemy, but I don't know if it's going to be worth adding points yet or waiting until we have a base somewhere. Or maybe I should wait and see if I manage to access some other skills. Like enchanting or leatherwork. Not that I have any clue on how to unlock them." She relaxed against Ryan, yawning. "Do you think if we all slept through the trip to Wayholt it'd upset the wagoner?" She spoke softly so her voice didn't carry to the front of the wagon.

Ryan chuckled. "Sleep if you want. I can stay awake. At least for an hour or so. Then you can take a turn watching and I can have a sleep."

She rested her head against his chest. "Next time we should work out the times better. It's going to take us a while to get into the sleeping pattern of this world."

"The problem is the time difference."

Chapter Ten

"Mmm." Mallory's eyes closed and she relaxed against Ryan, wishing there was space for her to lie down in the wagon. But there wasn't any extra room. Not that it mattered. Somehow she drifted off to sleep to be woken by Ryan, the wagon slowing to a stop.

"What's going on?" Brodie sat up, rubbing his eyes.

"There's a bear crossing the road about thirty metres ahead. If we're lucky it'll continue on its way," the wagoner said.

Brodie faced forward. "There's only one. Why don't we take it out while we've got surprise on our side?"

"A pity we don't have a spyglass to see how much health it has," Ryan said.

The wagoner took a brass spyglass out from underneath the timber seat. "Here."

Ryan raised the spyglass to his eye. "Twenty-five

health. We can take it. I can't see any others." He handed the spyglass back, jumping out of the wagon. "Might as well see what we can get. There's a bit of space left in the chest."

Mallory hopped off the wagon to stand beside Ryan, drawing her dagger and wand. "It can't be as bad as an undine."

Callum told Smudge to wait with the wagoner, readying his bow before walking towards the front of the wagon. "How about we don't talk or even think about her." He started to walk towards the bear. "I'm not so sure I want to set up our base near the coastline. Except I think Smudge would prefer it if we were near water. He loved playing in the ocean."

"Do they live in lakes?" Brodie asked, receiving a shrug for his answer.

Mallory followed Callum to the front of the wagon. They needed to be closer before they attacked. She glanced at the wagoner as she passed him. "How far are we from Wayholt?"

"We're a little over halfway."

She inclined her head, continuing to follow Callum who walked further along the road, Ryan on one side of her, Brodie on the other. They were less than an hour and a half from Buckneth. Not nearly enough sleep, but she supposed she shouldn't sleep too much or she wouldn't sleep tonight. She looked towards Ryan. "You can sleep the rest of the way if you want." She grinned. "Once we've dealt with the bear."

As if it heard her mention it, the bear raised its head and looked in their direction. It lumbered towards them, calling out in pain when an arrow pierced its body.

Mallory launched a fireball at the bear, managing to get in a second one before it came close. She hadn't realised it was moving so fast. It rose above her, opening its mouth to roar. Ryan jumped in front of the bear, attacking with his sword, preventing the bear from reaching her. She stumbled backwards, about to launch another fireball at the creature when it slumped on the ground after one last roar. She stared at the creature on the ground, blood staining the dirt, her heart still racing.

Callum lowered his bow. "Ryan should skin it. It'd be good if we can get a bear pelt for the wagoner to sell for us."

Taking a deep breath, she tried to ignore the adrenaline coursing through her body, bending to help Ryan skin the bear. Before she could draw her dagger, a yelp had her looking further up the road. "What was that?" She couldn't see anything that might have made the noise.

"Only one way to find out." Ryan waved the wagoner back and strode forward, a curve in the road preventing them from seeing what had made the noise.

She hurried after Ryan. Her heart, which had barely managed to slow its pace, was once again racing. "Wait up. Who knows what the noise was."

"It sounded like something being hurt," Callum said.

"It could have been a bear being hurt and we're about to walk around the corner and discover something way more powerful than us." Mallory gestured towards the corner they were approaching.

"Sounded like a dog to me," Callum said.

"Have you heard all the sounds a bear makes when it's being hurt?" Mallory asked. "It could also yelp for all we know."

Brodie dropped back. "Have you forgotten I don't have a revive?"

"Not like we can forget with how often you remind us," Callum said.

"Even if you die, it won't be a permanent death." Ryan remained slightly ahead of the group.

"Yeah, but I don't want to respawn back home naked and with no gear. Where will we get the money to buy me new weapons?" Brodie asked.

Mallory laughed. "He has a point there. I don't want him to respawn naked. I don't think I could survive the trauma."

Callum's laughter was cut off when they came around the corner and saw three men attacking a wolf cub, the body of a wolf and two other cubs lying on the bloodstained ground. "Do you think they're bandits?"

Brodie remained behind them. "I dunno. They look better armed than bandits."

Ryan shrugged. "Could be higher level bandits."

"What are we going–" Mallory broke off when one of the men looked towards them and nudged the companion closest to him. It was too late to retreat.

The third man laughed, kicking the wolf cub as he drew a short sword. The cub tumbled across the ground, yelping.

Anger raced through Mallory, one hand curling into a fist, the other tightening around the wand she held. "Stop." She ran forward, Ryan grabbing hold of her arm before she could reach the men, drawing her back several steps.

"Go find your own fun." The archer took an arrow from his quiver, but for now, didn't ready his bow.

Logically Mallory knew the cub would one day

become a wolf, but that didn't stop her from saying, "Don't kill it."

"Are you serious? Why wouldn't we kill it?" The first warrior drew his short sword.

She tried not to focus on their weapons. "It's only a baby."

"You're bandits. What if we pay you for the cub?" Ryan asked.

The three of them laughed, sharing a look. The one with the bow spoke. "Bandits. Who'd want to be one of those weaklings?"

"We're hellions." The one who'd drawn his short sword first, took a step towards them. "And you're interrupting our fun."

An entire string of swear words ran through her head. They were screwed. They were facing minions of the dark forces. Enemies of the Guardians Of The Round Table. She fought the urge to run. She didn't want to end up with an arrow in her back.

Ryan grinned. "Then we have no need to buy it from you. We'll take it instead." He took a step forward. "That cub is ours."

"This can't be good," Brodie muttered.

Mallory felt like agreeing with him. Instead, she launched a fireball at the archer hellion who was drawing back an arrow. The arrow fell to the ground and he reached for a second one. Beside her, Callum fired at one of the warrior hellions while Brodie remained at her shoulder throwing knives at the second warrior hellion who attacked Ryan. She threw another fireball at the archer before he could ready his bow. Launching fireball after fireball, she tried to keep him from attacking her, unable to focus on anything other than the archer hellion. If one of his arrows struck her, she doubted she'd survive.

"Mallory!"

At her brother's warning, she threw a final fireball at the archer, who collapsed to the ground, and turned to see the warrior hellion come in from her left. She didn't have time to block or dodge. Pain shot through her side, the shouts of her companions and the barking of the cub fading. The pain travelled through her entire body until all she could feel was an explosion of pain. The world went black. Sensation faded. There was nothing.

Chapter Eleven

The world came into focus, but Mallory couldn't move. The pain had ended, but it felt like it remained, the memory burned into her brain. She tried to move. It was impossible. Then she could. Thoughts seemed frozen and she stared at the scene in a daze.

Ryan wrapped his arms around her. "You okay?"

She wasn't sure. She felt disconnected from her body, like it wasn't quite hers. "He one-hit me." Nearby she could hear the cub growling. She clung to Ryan, trying to ignore the phantom feeling of pain.

Brodie moved closer. "I tried to stop him." He clutched his stiletto. "He was too quick. I was busy attacking the other hellion so I didn't notice him until it was too late."

She slowly let go of Ryan, stepping away from

him, trying to centre herself. "They're dead?" She glanced around the area.

Callum nodded. "The wolf cub went after the one that killed you."

Mallory shuddered, her mind shying away from his words. "How about we don't mention that again." It wasn't a sensation she wanted to repeat. Or focus on. Her gaze was drawn to the cub that was attacking the leg of one of the dead hellions. She didn't blame the creature. "What are we going to do with it?"

Brodie slowly moved closer to the cub, crouching as he drew near. "It's kind of cute." He held out his hand. "Come here." He spoke softly.

The cub turned to face him.

"Come on." He continued to hold out his hand, inching closer.

The cub sniffed his hand, licking his fingers.

Brodie laughed, causing the cub to shrink back. "Sorry. That felt funny." He carefully moved forward a bit, managing to pat the cub.

Again the cub licked his fingers.

"We should search the hellions," Callum said.

"And skin the wolf," Ryan suggested.

Brodie managed to pick up the cub, cradling it close. "That's probably the cub's mum. You can't do that. Not in front of it." He smiled down at the cub. "It's a girl."

"What are we going to do with her?" Callum searched one of the hellions.

Brodie grinned. "Keep her. Did you see how she attacked the hellions?" He looked at his hand, blood on it. "They hurt her." He glared at the closest hellion. "Lucky he's dead or I'd make him regret it."

Mallory joined her brother, patting the cub. If they left her behind, she wouldn't survive. "How will she be any different to a wild wolf? What if she turns on us when she grows up? We need to ask someone."

"Wolves can be trained, like dogs," Callum said. "And we can't leave her behind. She's too young to look after herself."

Mallory nodded. "I suppose we can ask someone later. It's not like she'll grow up overnight." At least she hoped the cub wouldn't. She looked at her brother. "What are you going to call her?" The cub was a mixture of colours. Her legs were mostly white, the rest of her grey, with some red amongst it, along with a few white sections. She stared into the blue eyes, a hint of amber tones in them. "You are very cute."

"I don't know. Did you see how she went for them hellions?" Brodie asked.

"Planning to cause some mayhem before she died," Ryan said. "How about May?"

Brodie shook his head. "That's lame."

"How about naming her for the colour of her fur?" Mallory asked.

"Coral? Honey?" Ryan asked.

"What about caramel? Or candy?" Mallory continued to pat the cub, smiling when the cub licked her fingers.

"Now I'm getting hungry," Brodie muttered.

"Snowy?" Mallory and Ryan said at the same time, both laughing.

"Dawn?" Callum suggested.

"Jewel?" Ryan gave four arrows to Callum, that he found on the archer hellion.

"Thanks. I lost one in that fight." Callum turned to Brodie. "What about sweetie? Look at that face." He slipped an arrow into his quiver before adding the rest to the spare arrows tied on the outside of the quiver.

"That's lame," Brodie said. "All your suggestions are lame. Look at her teeth. She's going to be a fighter. I bet she'll fight right alongside us." He stared at the cub for a moment. "Fang. That's what I'll call her."

Ryan grinned. "Fang."

"Yes," Brodie stated. "Fang." He looked into the cub's eyes. "I accept companion animal Fang."

"I think it might take a bit for her to grow into that name," Mallory said.

"But she will grow into it," Brodie said.

"I'll move these bodies off the road and then we'll check on the wagoner and finish seeing what we can get from the bear." Ryan hoisted the archer hellion onto his shoulder.

Mallory's gaze was drawn to the hellion's hand. There was a tattoo of a skull with dark eye sockets, the edges partially obscured by tendrils of smoke.

Ryan looked down at the hellion that he dumped on the side of the road, looking between him and Mallory. "They all have that tattoo. The others have them on their chest."

"What did we get from them?" Brodie asked.

"As well as the arrows, we got a tunic, one silver piece, two copper pieces and a belt pouch." Callum carried the dead cubs to the side of the road.

Fang whined.

Brodie patted her. "It's okay, girl. You've got us now." When Fang stopped whining, he asked, "Can I have the belt pouch? I could keep snacks in it. Like berries and jerky."

"Will they last long enough for you to need

somewhere to store them?" Grinning, Ryan held out the pouch.

"Very funny." Brodie took the pouch, setting Fang on the ground beside him so he could add it to his belt. The cub stared up at him.

Sheathing her dagger, Mallory picked up the brown tunic. "What's with all the tunic drops? What about trousers?"

Finished moving bodies from the road, Ryan took the tunic from her. "At the rate ours get sliced up, we're going to need them." He slung it over his shoulder and took her hand. "You okay?" He looked her up and down.

She shrugged. "I suppose so." At least she no longer felt like her body should be in pain or that it belonged to someone else. "Is everyone else okay?" She checked the stats in the journal. "Callum! Have a potion." He only had five health points left.

"I was thinking I might get an hour's sleep on the way to Wayholt," Callum said.

Mallory slipped her wand into the canvas loop and held out her health potion. "That'll only give you a single point. We can't be much past midday. That's too long to go with low health."

Ryan shook his head, stepping between her and Callum. "Have this one." He gave his health potion to Callum, who drank it and put the empty vial in his pocket.

Mallory returned the health potion to her pocket, checking the stats once more. Callum's health was back to fifteen. The potions were either instant or fairly close to being instant.

Brodie carried Fang when they headed towards the wagon. "Do you think she's old enough to eat yet?"

"She looks to be about five-weeks-old. Her eyes are still blue. They'll change to a yellowish gold colour any time from eight-weeks-old," Callum said. "She's probably having mother's milk, but able to feed on her own too if you cut the meat up small for her."

"How do you know?" Brodie asked.

"I watched a documentary on wolves last year. They're really interesting creatures," Callum said.

Chapter Twelve

They stopped at the bear, able to see that the wagoner was unharmed, Smudge sitting in the seat beside him. They left it to Ryan to skin the bear, Mallory helping him. Callum managed to get two bear canines and Ryan six kilograms of meat as well as a pelt.

Brodie grinned when Fang chewed on the bear carcass. "We should get a couple of bones for her."

"You better not be planning to feed her in the wagon," Callum said.

"I can wrap them in a piece of that canvas in the backpack and give them to her later." Brodie tried to hack bones off with his stiletto.

Ryan moved him out of the way and used his short sword, handing over two meaty bones. They returned to the wagon where Smudge greeted them excitedly and Callum put the empty vial into the backpack. After washing their hands, Ryan and

Mallory put the pelt and canines in the chest, for the wagoner to sell, before clambering onto the wagon. Before getting comfortable, they wrapped the meat in some canvas and put it in the backpack.

"I'd begun to think you weren't coming back," the wagoner said.

Callum warily watched Fang and Smudge greet each other. "We ran into some hellions."

The wagoner, who'd started the horses moving, looked over his shoulder. "Should we turn back?"

Ryan shook his head. "They won't be bothering anyone else."

Callum patted Smudge and Fang before lying down. "Wake me when we're nearly there."

Smudge chirped at Fang, patting her on the nose before turning and snuggling up with Callum.

Brodie grinned, gathering Fang close. "They're friends already. Did you see that?" Fang licked his face, causing him to laugh.

Mallory noticed a clump of herbs a couple of metres from the side of the road. "Why are there so many herbs to be collected the moment you leave a village?"

"People don't stray far from towns and villages. Too many dangerous creatures, bandits and rogues. Some more venturous souls wander away from settlements alone, but most don't want to risk it. So there's always a market for those who are willing to gather herbs, and other resources, from the wild," the wagoner said.

"We should gather them." Mallory grinned, turning to Ryan. "After all you and I are falling behind on XP. I've only got twenty-four and you've got twenty-five. They've got twenty-nine and thirty. Callum has the most." She paused a moment. "Unless you want a sleep."

Ryan chuckled. "You're sounding like your brother." He glanced at another cluster of herbs they passed. "Only the ones not far from the road." He hopped off the back of the wagon. "Coming?"

They spent the next three quarters of an hour gathering enough herbs to bring their experience points up to thirty, Brodie collecting two herbs. Mallory clambered back onto the wagon, leaning against Ryan when he joined her. "That probably wasn't a good idea. If we run into danger I doubt I could do much. I'm exhausted from all the running back and forth."

"After a few minutes rest we'll be good," Ryan said. "Our stamina is low."

Mallory brought up her journal. "I didn't think to check that." As she watched, five stamina returned.

Brodie patted Fang, throwing two apple cores over the side of the wagon. "We should get her a studded collar. To protect her neck when she fights. And some armour when she's bigger." He stared down at her. "Do you think Mum would mind if I brought her home when we return?"

"She'd want to take her to the RSPCA," Mallory said.

"What if she misses me while we're gone?" Brodie asked.

Mallory couldn't resist smiling. "We probably won't go for very long at a time." She looked from Fang to Smudge and back again. "I doubt Callum will want to be parted from his companion animal long either."

The wagoner slowed the horses. "This could be a trap."

Mallory turned to see what was ahead, about to ask the wagoner what he meant. Her mouth remained open as she stared at the man who walked along the side of the road, turning to face them. He held broken branches in front of and behind himself, appearing to be completely naked behind the leaves.

Brodie laughed. "We've only got tunics to lend him." He laughed again.

"He's not overly large. Not much taller than

Mallory. Either tunic should be long enough for him to cover the essentials." Ryan grinned.

Mallory slowly shook her head. "Surely this isn't a trap. Why would someone walk naked along the side of the road as part of a trap?"

"Remain vigilant," the wagoner said softly.

Ryan jumped off the back of the wagon. "Wake Callum."

The wagoner drew to a stop. "What seems to be the problem?"

The man remained at a distance. "I was attacked by bandits about fifteen minutes ago. You going to Wayholt?"

"Need a lift?" The wagoner nodded to the broad seat of the wagon.

"Ah, well…" The man glanced at Mallory.

She rummaged in the backpack and held out the army green tunic they'd taken from the bandits on the beach. "We can lend you this."

"Ah, I appreciate it, but…" He glanced down.

Ryan chuckled, taking the tunic from Mallory. "Turn around." He grinned at her before striding to the man.

She turned her back on the man, hearing the rustle of leaves. "How many bandits attacked you?"

"Three of them." The man paused a moment. "You

can turn around now. Thanks for sparing my dignity."

Mallory turned in time to see him sit beside the wagoner. "Where do you live?"

The man shifted on the seat so he could face Mallory. "Across the road from the cobbler. I work evenings at the tavern. Cook's assistant."

"Do you know the girl who brings the beef and vegetable pasties?" Brodie asked.

The cook's assistant nodded. "She tends to bring a basket of them around midday and around sunset in time for the evening meal. Occasionally, if it's busy, the tavern owner will send someone around to ask her to bring an extra lot during the afternoon. I hear she's planning to head back up north to her father."

"So she'll be there at sunset today," Brodie said.

The cook's assistant nodded. "How do you know Danae?"

"Uhmm…" Brodie's voice trailed off.

Mallory took pity on her brother. "We met her last time we were in Wayholt."

"You travel around the countryside a bit?" The cook's assistant continued when they nodded. "Then maybe you can help me. I need someone to get my gear back from the bandits. I heard them say they were heading to their hut. As long as I get my gear you're welcome to whatever else you find."

"What did they take?" Ryan asked.

"My clothes, boots, belt, belt pouch, two silver pieces and a recipe." The cook's assistant looked at each of them. "I really need that recipe. It's my chance to prove I can be more than an assistant."

Ryan glanced at his companions. Mallory smiled, Brodie shrugged and Callum nodded. He faced the cook's assistant. "We'll see what we can do."

Mallory checked her journal, smiling when she read the new quest. *Restore The Assistant's Dignity: Track down the bandits and return the items they stole from the cook's assistant.* She counted the active quests. Five. They were piling up again. When Ryan chuckled she glanced at him, wondering if he was also amused by the quest title.

They reached Wayholt a little after two-thirty, according to the wagoner, Brodie muttering about how long it had been since he'd eaten. The wagoner pulled up in front of the assistant's home and they got out of the wagon, making plans to meet at the tavern at sunset, leaving the shield and fishing pole in the wagon to collect later.

The cook's assistant remained on the doorstep of his timber cottage. "I'll draw a map of where the bandits' hut is from what they said. They thought I was unconscious, but I was only dazed. You're welcome to wait inside if you want." He looked to Brodie. "I have some bread left from the loaf I baked yesterday and honey to put on it."

Brodie brightened. "Sounds good." He followed the cook's assistant inside.

Grinning, Mallory trailed after her brother, slowly shaking her head.

Ryan moved close to Mallory to whisper in her ear. "Did you ever worry some stranger would entice your brother into his car, with food, when he was younger?"

"Mum and Dad tell stories about him joining random people's picnics when they took him to the park when he was a toddler."

Ryan chuckled. "That doesn't surprise me."

"What's funny?" Brodie asked.

Chapter Thirteen

Mallory tried not to laugh. She was unsuccessful, earning a glare from her brother.

The cook's assistant made his way to a table that took up a corner of the room. He unwrapped a calico cloth from a loaf of bread that was on the table, cutting it into thick slices. He nodded to a set of timber shelves next to the table. "Grab plates and the honey off the top shelf."

Brodie set Fang down and collected the plates and honey.

Callum put Smudge beside the cub, smiling when the river otter patted the wolf cub. "They're very cute together. I wasn't sure they'd get along." He shrugged. "I guess things aren't quite the same here."

"It might have something to do with them both being companion animals," Ryan said.

Mallory took the plate Brodie handed her, two

slices of bread spread with honey. "Thanks." She looked around. There was only a bench seat by the table and Brodie and Callum sat on it, no space for anyone else. The cottage didn't have much, but unlike many of the cottages in Buckneth this one had a paved stone floor. In the middle of the room was a fire pit, and on the far side was an open door. The second room had a double bed, the frame made of timber, a chest in the corner and a small table next to it with several pieces of parchment on it.

While they ate, the cook's assistant retreated to the second room, closing the door. When he came out, dressed in trousers and a blue tunic with no belt or boots, he returned the borrowed tunic. He held out a torn off piece of parchment with a crude map on it. "I appreciate your help. I think it's getting worse out on the roads."

Ryan took the map. "What is the recipe they took from you?"

"Rich herb gravy. It's only a low level recipe, but it can dramatically improve a roast dinner. As well as several other meals. I can write out a copy of the recipe for you when you return it," he offered.

"That sounds good," Brodie said.

Mallory shared a look with Ryan, returning his grin. Trying to make her expression more serious, she turned to the cook's assistant. "We better get started before it becomes too late to go after them."

Callum and Brodie gathered their companion animals and they headed out of Wayholt. Ryan frequently referred to the crude map. About twenty minutes into the journey Fang growled low. A few metres later they saw a thatched hut. They remained amongst the trees, examining the hut in the small clearing. Voices drifted through the open window, arguing over how to split their latest spoils.

"Are we going to attack?" Brodie asked. "I want to be at the tavern before sunset."

"I want to be back in Wayholt before the shops shut." Mallory took out her dagger and wand. "I need to buy a notebook. If I can find one that's not too expensive."

"You're not wasting money on a notebook," Brodie said. "Just because Kern thinks it's a good idea, doesn't mean it is. Ewen doesn't think it's necessary."

"I'll circle around the clearing. The door is on the other side. I can see it through the window." Ryan drew his sword. "Give me a few minutes to get in place then attack whichever bandit you see through the window." He took several steps away before he stopped and looked over his shoulder. "A notebook is a good idea. We're basically living two lives. We need some way of keeping track of everything."

Mallory watched him stride away before returning her attention to the hut. "There are so many things we need." Somehow they'd find a way to be better equipped. She just wasn't sure how.

"Exactly. We need lots of things. So you're not wasting our money on a notebook. Your memory isn't that bad." Brodie put Fang on the ground next to him and took out two throwing knives.

Callum readied his bow, Smudge on the ground beside him. "Three against one, Brodie."

Brodie muttered under his breath.

Mallory grinned, only catching a few of the words. They were more than enough to let her know how unimpressed he was. "Should we attack the next one that walks past the window?"

"Yeah," Callum said, echoed by Brodie.

She watched the window, waiting. "Where are they? Before they were walking back and forth all the time."

"You don't think they've caught Ryan, do you?" Callum asked.

Mallory didn't get the chance to answer. A bandit walked past the window. "Attack." She only had the opportunity to throw a single fireball at him. Brodie rapidly threw two knives and it was Callum's second arrow that took the bandit down.

"They're escaping," Ryan called out from the other side of the hut.

Mallory broke into a run, soon left behind by Brodie and Callum. Even their companion animals were faster than her. Reaching the corner of the hut, she threw a fireball at each of the bandits Ryan fought. Ryan finished off one and her third fireball finished off the last one. She remained by the corner of the hut, scanning the area, heart racing, body tense. Nothing moved.

"It seems clear." Callum lowered his bow.

"I'll search the hut. Someone else can search the bodies for a change." Brodie strode inside, Fang at his heels.

Mallory checked everyone's health. Only Ryan had lost any. Another three, bringing his health down to thirteen. She couldn't wait until her health was higher so small health losses didn't seem like such a big problem. And she wasn't as likely to be one-hit. A shudder ran through her and she tried not to think about dying. Seeing Ryan and Callum were searching the two bandits outside, she followed Brodie inside.

"They've got a feather pillow." Brodie held up the object, the material stained.

Mallory winced. "You're not going to keep it, are you?"

"We could wash it. Got to be better than sleeping on only a blanket." Brodie set the pillow back on the single bed in the hut. "There's a blanket too." He took the thin, stained blanket off the bed. He grinned. "It can be washed."

She glanced around the hut, the dirt floor darkened by blood from the bandit slumped on the floor by the window. There was a small campfire in the middle of the hut, three wooden bowls and wooden spoons sitting by it. Fang was sniffing under the bed, a hessian bag lying on top of the lumpy mattress. "There isn't much in here."

Ryan strode inside. "We got a cure disease potion and five copper pieces off them." He gave the potion and coins to Mallory. "What did you find?"

Fang scratched at the ground under the bed, whining.

"Help me move the bed out of the way." Brodie stood at one end, taking hold of the narrow timber frame.

Ryan went to the other end and helped Brodie shift it. "I wonder what she's found." He crouched beside Fang. "There's a bit of timber covered by dirt." He lifted the timber, the dirt falling off it.

Mallory moved closer, laughing when she saw the thirty grams of beef jerky. "She's definitely Brodie's companion."

"There's also a health potion and three silver pieces," Ryan said.

"You keep the potion." Mallory took the coins from him.

They found a dagger on the other bandit and took the three bowls and spoons as well as the hessian bag containing the gear belonging to the cook's assistant. The blanket, pillow, bowls and spoons were jammed into the basket, Ryan not wanting to put the gear in the backpack until it was cleaned.

Brodie scooped up Fang. "Does that mean I get the jerky since Fang found it?"

Ryan laughed as they headed outside. "Nice try."

"But it was my companion that found it. She should at least get some," Brodie protested.

"She can have some of the bear meat we got earlier," Ryan said. "The jerky will keep longer."

"Did someone check that all the assistant's gear is in that hessian bag?" Callum asked.

"I did," Mallory said. "Everything's in it." She carried the sack while Ryan carried the basket and the backpack.

"How long do you think it will be before the sun sets?" Brodie glanced at the sky.

Ryan shrugged. "A couple of hours at the most."

"I hope the shops don't shut early," Mallory said.

"You're not buying a notebook," Brodie stated.

Mallory grinned. "Three against one."

Brodie glared at them. "Why doesn't anyone ever agree with me?" He strode ahead when everyone laughed.

Chapter Fourteen

Mallory was relieved to return to Wayholt without running into any problems. She didn't want to risk Ryan's health getting lower. As it was, half their party no longer had revives. Half the human members of their party that was. If she counted the companion animals then less than half the party had revives.

Brodie reached the cottage first and knocked on the door. It was opened almost instantly.

The cook's assistant looked at each of them. "Did you find the bandits?" When they nodded, he asked, "What about my things? Were you able to find the recipe?"

Mallory handed over the hessian bag. "Everything is in there. Including the recipe."

The cook's assistant smiled broadly. "Thank you. I'll copy out the recipe for you." He took a step backwards. "Did you want to come in while I work on it?" He gestured towards a pot sitting over the fire. "I put a stew on while you were gone. It could do with a bit longer, but it's cooked enough if you want some now. I cut everything up small so it'd cook quicker."

"Yes. I'm starving." Brodie followed the cook's assistant inside.

Mallory once again shared a look with Ryan, returning his grin before she followed her brother. They helped themselves to the stew, finished eating by the time the cook's assistant returned to the main room, holding out a piece of parchment with small, neat handwriting covering it.

"I can give you a silver coin for your help or I have a storage basket with random items from when I was trying to decide on a career to pursue. I eventually decided cooking was for me, but I went through a few jobs first." The cook's assistant gestured towards a tall, woven straw basket in the corner. "Which would you prefer?"

Brodie turned to his sister. "We should take the money."

"Can we see what's in the basket?" Callum asked.

The cook's assistant nodded, once again gesturing towards the basket. "By all means. Have a look and make your decision."

"I didn't know we could look," Brodie said.

Mallory crossed the room, lifting the lid off the basket and peering inside. There was a hatchet with a leather loop so it could be hung from a belt, pruning shears in a leather case, a hand drum, hammer, saw, needle, thread and a drop spindle. She kept her voice low, her companions having crowded in around her. "These could unlock different crafting abilities. Who knows how much they'd normally cost."

"You only want them because there are pruning shears for your alchemy," Brodie said.

"I agree with Mallory," Ryan said.

Brodie turned to Callum. "Let me guess. You agree too."

Callum laughed softly. "Even if we don't want to keep all of this gear we might get more for it by selling it in a bigger town."

Brodie's gaze returned to the storage basket. "Okay. We'll take the junk."

Mallory faced the cook's assistant. "We'll take the items."

"Marvellous." The cook's assistant smiled. "They're all yours."

Once they'd gathered the gear, everything going in the backpack except the axe, which Ryan hung on his belt at his left hip, they headed outside. Mallory checked the updated quest, reading it aloud once the cottage door was shut. "Restore The Assistant's Dignity: The cook's assistant was relieved by the return of his items. You were rewarded with a hatchet, pruning shears, hand drum, hammer, saw, needle, thread, drop spindle and a recipe for rich herb gravy for your party. You also earned fifteen experience points each." She checked her stats. "I've got fifty-four XP. Over halfway to my next CAS point." She checked everyone else's stats. "We've all got fifty-four except Ryan."

"He can pick some herbs," Brodie said.

Ryan chuckled. "Why do I get the feeling you enjoyed saying that?"

Brodie grinned. "Me?"

"We've got two rep in Wayholt," Callum said.

"That's not bad considering how much time we've spent here," Ryan said.

They strode towards the trading post, finding a well beside the tavern to wash the gear they'd taken from the bandits. Brodie helped Callum wring out the pillow. "It's not going to be dry by tonight." Brodie returned the pillow to the basket. "I was looking forward to using it."

Finished at the well, Mallory looked along the road. "We should see what the trading post has."

It didn't take long to figure out that they couldn't afford the leather-bound notebook at the trading post. It was ten gold pieces. They only had six silver and seventeen copper pieces. Before they headed to the secondhand shop, Callum asked the shopkeeper if they sold coffee. He wasn't happy with the reply. He was also disappointed to learn that they didn't have any vambraces for sale.

When they entered the secondhand shop, Callum asked the same questions while Mallory searched the stock.

The shopkeeper shook his head. "We don't have any vambraces and I've never heard of the other. Is there something else I can help you with?"

"A notebook?" Callum asked.

"I don't know that you'll be interested. The moment anyone learns the first ten pages have been cut out, and there's only ninety left, they don't seem to be interested. I'll take two gold pieces for it."

Mallory sighed. "We can't afford it."

Smudge stood up beside her, holding out his pearl.

"I can't take that, Smudge. It's yours," Mallory said.

Smudge chirruped, continuing to hold it out to her.

"I couldn't afford it," the shopkeeper said. "I'd need

to give you three gold in change. I could manage to give you a single gold, but that's it."

Ryan turned to Mallory. "We could get some clothes, a hairbrush and that satchel that's only five silver pieces. We need more things for storing items."

Along with the notebook they bought a nearly empty bottle of ink with a wooden pen that had a metal nib. They also bought the satchel and a belt pouch that Ryan slipped onto his belt, giving the satchel to Mallory. She put the hairbrush into her satchel, along with the notebook, pen and ink. They purchased a thin blanket that looked as well used as the one from the bandits along with two pairs of basic trousers and a black tunic. She handed over the pearl and the shopkeeper gave her a gold coin in change.

"Where did you get the pearl?" the shopkeeper asked.

"In the ocean west of Buckneth," Brodie said.

"You found the sunken ship?" the shopkeeper asked.

"What sunken ship?" Callum asked.

"What's in it?" Brodie spoke at the same time as Callum.

The shopkeeper looked at each of them. "You haven't heard about it? Apparently one of the scholars at the Mages Guild in Shadhurst recently discovered mention of it in an old book. No one knows exactly where it is other than it went down on the western side of Ruby Isle. Not even the merfolk seem to know. Or if they do, they aren't saying anything."

"What's so important about it?" Brodie asked.

"There's an enchanted mage staff on board." The shopkeeper turned to Mallory, nodding to her wand. "Thought you might have gone looking for it being a mage."

"Now that sounds like something that'd be valuable," Brodie said.

The shopkeeper nodded. "Valuable enough that once the dark forces learn about it they'll probably look for it too."

Thanking the shopkeeper, they headed outside, Brodie grumbling, wanting to learn more about the sunken ship. Mallory looked down at Smudge. "Thank you. We'll keep that gold piece to buy something for you."

Smudge yipped a couple of times and mimed eating.

Callum laughed, taking the fish out of the backpack and cutting off a piece for Smudge. When Fang barked, they had to cut up small pieces of bear meat for her.

Noticing a journal icon in the corner of her vision,

Mallory checked. "We have a new quest." She grinned. "One that will suit Brodie."

Ryan chuckled. "Can't argue that."

Chapter Fifteen

Mallory read the quest aloud. "Hunt For Enchanted Staff: Locate the lost staff before the dark forces learn its location. If the merfolk know the location they are keeping it to themselves, but most believe the ship is probably in one of the areas they avoid."

Brodie patted Fang. "Where do they avoid? If it was shallow water someone would have seen the ship."

"Not if it's been there a long time and has sunk into the sand," Ryan said.

Mallory thought of the merfolk they'd seen that morning. "Undines."

"What?" Brodie asked.

Callum nodded. "Makes sense. Merfolk aren't going to go anywhere undines hang out."

"How are we going to get past an undine?" Brodie demanded. "Or a group of them."

"Better yet, how are we meant to breathe underwater?" Ryan asked.

"Don't tell me it's another quest we're too low for," Brodie muttered.

Mallory shrugged. "Who knows."

Brodie started along the road. "Might as well wait at the tavern for Danae to turn up."

Ryan caught up with him. "We need to find somewhere to set up camp tonight. We don't want to be looking for a place in the dark."

Brodie muttered under his breath, his muttering increasing when they walked past the tavern. It was late afternoon by the time they found a suitable location. It was out past the apothecary's shop and south of the orchards. They draped the blanket over a low tree and placed the pillow on a bush to give them time to dry. Before they headed to the tavern they gathered firewood and left it stacked in a neat pile near the fire pit they'd prepared.

Mallory took one last look at where they'd sleep that night. "Are you sure it's safe to leave the blanket and pillow behind?"

Ryan shrugged. "If we keep carting them around bundled up they're not going to dry and will end up mouldy." He changed into the black tunic. The other two dressed in the trousers and tunics, both finding a broad tree to stand behind. Brodie wore the army green tunic.

Mallory looked them over when they returned to the campsite. She smiled. "You're starting to look like you belong here." Her smile faded. "I want clothes that suit this place."

"You've got boots." Brodie pointed to them.

"We'll get you a tunic next," Ryan said.

They returned to Wayholt, arriving at the tavern before the sun set. The wagoner rose from the table where he sat, waving them over. They joined him at the table, barely sitting down before he dropped a pile of silver coins in front of Mallory.

She counted them, smiling. "Thank you."

"How many?" Brodie asked.

"Fifteen." She pocketed them, happy with their earnings. "You were able to sell everything?"

The wagoner nodded. "What time do you want to go to the mine tomorrow morning?"

A man at the table next to them turned in his seat. He had greenish grey skin, bulging arm muscles and protruding lower canines. He was dressed in leather trousers and boots and wore a hide vest. "You're going to the mine?"

"Better not be another quest," Brodie muttered. "We've already got too many."

Mallory tried not to laugh at her brother, but she couldn't prevent a smile from forming. She looked over at the man, trying to figure out what he was. "Yeah. We're going to South Peak Mine tomorrow."

"Do you think you can take a letter for me? I need to get a message to my brother. Kruth Blackhelm. He hasn't replied to the last letter I sent so I need someone who'll deliver one directly to him."

"Finally. Something simple," Brodie said.

"He's one of the guards at South Peak Mine and we haven't heard from him since the goblin troubles started," the man said.

"Maybe not so simple," Ryan said.

"Can you help me out?" the man asked.

"Give us a minute to discuss it," Ryan said.

The man nodded, his gaze remaining on them.

Brodie leaned forward, keeping his voice low. "What happens if the goblins killed his brother? Does that mean we'll be stuck with a quest we can't finish?"

Mallory shook her head, speaking as quietly as her brother. "It means we become the bearer of bad news." She looked towards the wagoner, keeping her voice as low as possible. "What race is he?"

"Orc."

Mallory started to say she thought orcs were a

darker green, but remained silent in case the orc could hear her.

Ryan glanced at each of them. "We're doing it then?"

"Yeah," Mallory said, echoed by Callum and Brodie. She turned to the orc. "We can take a letter to your brother."

The orc rose from his seat, towering over them. "Thank you." He held out his hand. "I'm Grotmur Blackhelm."

Mallory looked up at him. He had to be at least six and a half feet tall. She stood, not liking how he loomed over her. She shook his hand. "I'm Mallory Owens." She introduced the rest of her party.

"I'll be back in about twenty minutes with the letter. I really appreciate this." Grotmur hurried from the tavern.

Sitting, Mallory checked her journal, reading the quest aloud. "Missing Guard: Grotmur Blackhelm needs a letter delivered to his brother as he has not heard from him since the goblin troubles started at South Peak Mine."

"Missing guard." Brodie frowned. "That doesn't sound good."

"If you don't mind delivering letters," the wagoner said. "And you have someone to vouch for you or you've proven yourself in that area, you can check with taverns for any mail that needs delivering. You can earn a copper piece, or more depending on the distance, for each letter you take to the town or village you're travelling to. I've already collected the ones from here, but it might be worth keeping in mind during your travels. I can vouch for you at the tavern in Surith if you plan to travel around a bit once you've escorted me home."

"Thanks," Ryan said.

Brodie grabbed Callum's arm. "She's here." Fang, who'd been curled up asleep in Brodie's lap, lifted her head and looked around.

Mallory turned towards the door, smiling when she saw Danae had entered with a basket. Today her long blond hair was braided back from her face, her pointed ears clearly visible. "Are you going to say hello?" She watched as Danae made her way to the bar, smiling at the bartender as she handed over the basket.

"If you don't hurry up she'll be gone before you have the chance to talk to her," Ryan warned.

Brodie turned to Callum. "Give me Smudge."

"Take Fang with you." Callum grinned. "Since you need a companion animal to hide behind."

Brodie rose, setting Fang on his seat. "I don't need

to hide behind anything or anyone." He strode towards Danae who was heading for the door, carrying her now empty basket.

Ryan chuckled. "Think he'll talk to her?"

"Until his burst of anger wears off," Callum said.

Mallory, who'd been watching Brodie talk to Danae, smiled when he looked in their direction several times. "Which is about now." Taking pity on her brother, she rose, waving the two of them over.

The wagoner also rose. "I'll leave you to it. Shall we meet here around daybreak?"

"Two hours after daybreak," Ryan suggested. "We'll need to cook food before we leave."

The wagoner nodded, heading for the door, giving Brodie a nod on his way past.

Brodie introduced them to Danae. "She needs an escort to Surith," he blurted out.

Chapter Sixteen

Mallory stared at Danae's pale green eyes, so light in colour that they reminded her of how pale Richelle's eyes were.

"Most people call me Danni. Except for my mother and her customers." Danae sat in the seat the wagoner had vacated. "And I don't exactly need to go to Surith. I need to go to Simria, but I can catch a ship from Surith. I was meant to leave a couple of weeks ago, just after my sixteenth birthday, which is the earliest you can apply to the Alchemy Academy. But no one seems to be travelling that way. I don't want to lose my place at the academy. I'm meant to be there within three months of my acceptance. At this rate, I'm never going to find someone to escort me back to my father so he can organise passage on a ship to Eridell for me."

"Your parents are divorced?" Callum asked.

"They never married to begin with. My father is a human and my mother an elf and they could never decide which culture they wanted to be married under." Danae smiled, shrugging. "Not that it matters now. My father was a peddler and when he earned enough money to buy his own general goods shop my mother didn't want to leave her hometown. So I've travelled between them for years. Although I usually spend more time in Simria than I do here. My father considered returning to Eridell, the country of his birth, but he decided he could make more money in Simria."

"What happened that you didn't leave after your sixteenth birthday?" Mallory asked.

"The ones who were going to escort me were offered a better paying job. They said they'd be back in about three weeks, but I'd rather not pay them to take me since they postponed the trip." Danae's attention was caught by Fang. "How many pets do you have? I'd love to have a pet of my own. Although I do have my father's horse he travelled around on when he was a peddler. But it's not the same. She prefers my father over me."

"She's my companion," Brodie said.

Danae's hand stilled on Fang's head. "She is?" She met Brodie's gaze. "What's it like? I've never been in a party or had the chance to have a companion animal."

Brodie shrugged, looking uncomfortable.

Once again Mallory took pity on him. After all, he hadn't really had Fang long enough to answer that. "Did Brodie explain we need to travel to South Peak Mine tomorrow? There's a quest we want to do and a letter we need to deliver to Grotmur Blackhelm's brother."

Danae's eyes widened. "A quest. I've always wanted to go on a quest. Just once to see what it's like. Well, maybe twice. You'd probably need to do something more than once to really know what it's like." She turned to Brodie. "Can I join you?"

"Sure," Brodie said.

"Now wait a minute–" Ryan began.

"I can make a health tea," Danae said.

"What is that?" Mallory asked.

"It's made with a mixture of herbs steeped in hot water. It gives you one health point for a cup of tea. I can teach you how to make it if you have level three alchemy," Danae said.

"That could be useful." Callum leaned forward, resting his arms on the table, his gaze meeting Mallory's. "And it won't take you long to get level three alchemy."

"We don't have a spare waterskin to store it in," Ryan said.

"The recipe and a two-litre waterskin. That's eight cups of health tea." Danae reached across the table to grab Mallory's hand. "Please. I used to beg my father to take me with him, but he always said it was too dangerous."

Mallory drew her hand from Danae's grip. "What will your mother say?" She really didn't need an elf annoyed with her for leading her daughter into danger.

"If you let me pick herbs along the way I can tell her I'm going on a herb gathering trip with you," Danae said.

"Come on, Mal," Brodie urged. "It's a low level quest. Even the mercs weren't interested in it."

Mallory looked from Danae to Brodie, sighing. She'd never hear the end of it if she said no.

Ryan chuckled. "Do you really think you have a choice, Mallory?"

A wry smile formed as Mallory met Ryan's gaze. "Probably not."

"Hell yeah!" Brodie grinned. "How do we do this?"

Danae grinned too. "The party leader has to accept me and then I can choose a class based on one of your classes." Her grin vanished. "Although I have no weapons. I suppose I could go unarmed." She laughed softly. "I put a point in unarmed when I unlocked it at fifteen. That taught the bullies in Simria not to mess with me."

Mallory stared at Danae. "There's unarmed combat?"

Danae nodded.

Callum punched Brodie in the arm. "That didn't unlock anything."

Brodie glared at Callum. "Hey."

Danae laughed. "You can't use your party members for training. It doesn't work like that." She turned to Mallory. "What classes do you have? Can you add me to the party now? I wouldn't be able to sleep tonight if you made me wait until morning. You can't believe how excited I am."

Mallory nodded. She could easily believe how excited Danae was. The half-elf was bursting with excitement. "Okay. I'll add you now. And we have warrior, mage, archer and rogue."

"That's good. Being part elf I'll have a bonus if I go archer." Danae's smile faded. "If I had a bow."

"We've got a spare short bow," Callum said. "And two spare daggers if you wanted to choose mage."

Mallory rested her hand on Danae's arm. "Accept party member Danae."

The half-elf grabbed Mallory's hands. "Thank you so much." She let go. "Choose class. Archer. It reset my attributes to class attributes. Not that my attributes were very good to start with." She flashed a grin at Brodie. "Meeting you was one of the best things to ever happen to me."

Brodie's face flushed. "Ahh…"

Ryan chuckled. "Give it time. You might end up changing your mind. Especially with how much he eats all the time."

"I'll bring some food when we meet up tomorrow. Beef and vegetable pasties. My mother won't mind. She always cooks extra." Danae stood up. "I'll wait until tomorrow to borrow the bow." She took a step away from the table. "If you're looking for more quests, have you checked the noticeboard? All kinds of things are posted there. From quests to jobs and even houses that are for sale."

"You can buy houses here?" Ryan asked.

Danae nodded. "Did you want me to show you where the noticeboard is before I leave?" When they nodded, she led them to a corner of the tavern.

Mallory immediately spotted a house for sale. "We're never going to afford a house. Look at this one. Timber house, thatch roof, two rooms, dirt floor, a thousand gold pieces."

"You don't have to worry about buying a house," Danae said. "You're adventurers. You can find land outside of a town or village and have someone build a house for you. Or build it yourself."

"How far out of a town?" Ryan asked.

"Two kilometres," Danae said. "Or you could find a village within a reasonable distance of a decent sized town that is on its way to becoming a ghost village. One suffering severe problems. Places there will be cheap and if you help the village grow, people will move there. Or return. You could also claim places through squatter's rights, but you need to be careful that someone doesn't come along wanting it back. Such as the original owner or a relative. It's usually not that hard to find the owner. They tend to move to the closest town or village."

"There's a house for rent." Callum pointed to one of the notices.

Danae nodded. "You could do that if you found a village in need of help. Buy up the cheap housing and rent them out when it improves."

"We could be real estate tycoons," Brodie exclaimed.

Ryan laughed. "I think we're a long way from that."

"There are all kinds of notices," Callum said.

Danae nodded. "A tavern is the heart of a town or village. People need somewhere to gather and share information." She turned to Mallory. "Did you want to share the information in our journals? Or don't you do that in your party?"

Chapter Seventeen

Mallory glanced around the group. Everyone nodded. "Yeah. We do share info." She smiled. "I forgot about it actually."

"Share journal information," Danae said.

"Share journal info." Brodie was the first to speak, echoed by Mallory, Ryan and Callum.

Danae took Brodie's hand, smiling at him. "I'll see you in the morning. Thank you for inviting me." With another smile for Brodie, and one for the rest of them, she headed for the door. She collected her basket, which she'd left at the table, along the way.

Ryan nodded towards the noticeboard. "This is good to know. We should never have a shortage of quests we can do."

"Are we buying dinner here?" Brodie asked.

Mallory grinned. Some things never changed. "We'll go back to our camp and cook something."

She walked towards the table where they'd left Smudge, Fang and their gear.

"Do you think bear meat is okay for humans to eat?" Callum gathered up Smudge.

"Fang likes it." Brodie picked up the cub, patting her on the head.

They stopped at the door, Ryan lighting the lantern before they stepped outside. "I don't see why it wouldn't be."

"I wonder if Smudge likes bear meat. He's nearly finished all that fish we kept. There's probably only one more meal of it left for him," Callum said.

"I don't know where we'll get fish around here if he doesn't eat bear meat." Mallory glanced around the area, night making it impossible to see far.

"At least now we've got a bowl each." Callum glanced at Brodie. "And you don't have to act like I'm about to steal your last mouthful every time I have some of my share."

Mallory walked beside Ryan, smiling as she listened to Brodie and Callum argue about food. "We've got carrots, potatoes and one onion. We could try making bear stew. That shouldn't be too difficult."

"You wouldn't think so, but who knows in this world. Breakfast didn't turn out as well as I'd expected. Fish isn't that hard to cook. I've cooked it plenty of times back home." Reaching the campsite, Ryan set down the lantern and worked on lighting the campfire.

Mallory diced up the vegetables while Callum and Brodie fed their companion animals, also giving Fang a bone to chew on. It didn't take long for them to have the bear stew cooking and Callum and Brodie returned to the village to refill the waterskin at the well.

Mallory stared off into the darkness. "Do you think we should have gone with them?"

"We're not that far out of the village. They should be okay." Ryan joined her by the fire.

She took the leather-bound notebook, pen and ink out of her satchel. "I should write something about our first few days while they're reasonably fresh in my mind."

Ryan grinned. "And before your brother returns to pay out on you."

"Or complain about the waste of coins." She opened the bottle of ink and turned to the first page of the notebook.

Ryan chuckled. "Probably both."

She stared at the blank page, not sure what to write. There were so many things that had happened. But if she wrote every little detail she'd soon run out of pages. She dipped the pen in the ink, tapping it against the top of the bottle.

Day One

Arriving on Ruby Isle, Inadon, with no clue where we were or what we were doing, we headed east to Buckneth. We completed some quests and met Ahron the tavern owner, the wagoner and his wife the baker, a hunter, Ninette, Osbert senior and junior, a weaver and Smudge a river otter. Completing a quest gave us two days free stay at the local tavern. We also met a shady character while questing and Brodie used up his revive when he was killed while we fought wolves.

Day Two

We escorted Ninette and Osbert junior to Wayholt, all the while thinking we had to hide from the guardians. They caught up with us at Ninette's home when we returned and we learned that they couldn't stop us from journeying to Inadon. We also learned that we have the opportunity to become guardians if we pass their test. Which is performance based.

Day Three

After buying Smudge and arranging for Ninette to look after him, we left our gear with Ahron and returned home in the morning. During the three days we were home we learned more about the guardians and returned to Inadon, arriving before ten in the evening of the same day we left.

Day Four

We escorted the wagoner to Wayholt and rescued Fang, a wolf cub, from hellions along the way. Brodie accepted her as his companion animal. This time I was the one to use up a revive during a fight. Danae, or Danni as she prefers to be called, has temporarily joined our party and will be going to South Peak Mine to complete the quest with us. We bought more equipment, but our party is still lacking gear and money.

Ryan chuckled, reading over her shoulder. "You forgot to mention that we're also lacking skills and experience."

She stared at her writing, a few ink spots scattered across the page. "Do you think I need to write more?"

Ryan shook his head. "That should be enough to remind us about everything."

Mallory smiled as she noticed the journal icon in the corner of her vision. "You have unlocked scribe, a crafting ability that allows you to make ink and parchment, draw maps, bind books and copy books." She held out the notebook and pen. "Did you want to unlock it?"

Ryan nodded, taking them from her and writing

his name on the inside of the cover. "That triggered it."

Before she could ask Ryan if they should be worried about their brothers, she heard them coming towards the campsite. The moment they were close enough, she asked if they wanted to unlock scribe too. Both added their name beneath Ryan's. Smiling, Mallory added her name there too, fitting it in above Ryan's name, before she put the bottle of ink away and cleaned the nib of the pen with a calico cloth Ryan handed her. The pen and calico went in her satchel and, after checking the ink was dry, she put the notebook away too.

Ryan moved closer to the fire, stirring the food. "This is smelling all right."

Brodie dropped onto the ground next to Mallory. Fang flopped down beside him, bringing her bone with her. "How long until it's ready?"

Ryan shrugged. "I've never made bear stew before."

"We should check out some of the gear we got from the cook's assistant," Callum said.

"Yeah, I want to play the drum." Brodie moved over to the backpack.

Callum groaned. "Now I'm wondering why I said anything."

Ryan and Mallory laughed, and she shared a look with Callum. "I think you only need to worry if he starts to sing."

"Very funny," Brodie muttered. He sat by the fire and tentatively hit the drum a couple of times. "Hey, that's all it takes to unlock bard."

Callum took the drum from him, hit it a couple of times then handed it along to Ryan who passed it on to Mallory once he'd used it.

"I wasn't finished with it," Brodie said.

Mallory hit the drum, the sound ringing out. Smiling, she checked the new message, frowning when Brodie took the drum from her and began to play. "You have unlocked bard, a crafting ability that allows you to evoke emotions in living things through playing musical instruments and singing." She winced when Brodie hit the drum harder. "I wonder if they mean emotions like annoyance."

Ryan chuckled. "Could also be murderous ones."

Brodie turned to face Ryan, opening his mouth to argue. An arrow missed him by millimetres. It would have hit him if he hadn't moved.

Fang started barking and Smudge made his high-pitched warning sound. The four of them jumped to their feet, reaching for weapons. Another arrow came towards Brodie, hitting a tree behind him.

Chapter Eighteen

Spotting two archer skeletons, Mallory threw a fireball at one of them. "Looks like you were right, Ryan. It does cause murderous emotions." She slowly moved to the side as she threw a fireball at the second archer skeleton, not wanting to be hit by an arrow.

Callum laughed, firing at each skeleton. "Can't say I blame them." He swore when an arrow pierced his arm, dropping the third arrow he'd taken from his quiver.

"Smudge should have let us know they were there." Brodie threw a knife at each skeleton, one of them missing. He threw a third knife at the skeleton he missed.

Ryan ran towards the skeletons. "He probably couldn't hear over your racket." He attacked one, spinning to attack the other. "And he wouldn't have been able to smell them either because the breeze is going in the wrong direction."

Mallory kept throwing fireballs at the skeletons, which were unable to attack now the four of them were fighting. Fang joined in, going for the one on the left. She growled as she attacked, Smudge bounding across the ground to help her. When the skeletons crumpled into piles of bone, Mallory checked everyone's stats, relieved to find Callum had only lost three health points. "No more playing drums." She slipped her wand back into the loop of canvas as she scanned the area. "It's not worth the response we get from the audience."

Ryan chuckled. "They're a tough crowd around here."

Brodie glared at his sister. "They didn't attack because of my playing." He gathered his throwing knives, stopping to pat Fang. "If we had Danni's tea Callum could heal himself."

Callum gathered his arrows once he checked Smudge over. "I don't think I could drink three cups of tea. And if I did, I'd probably be waking up, on and off all night, for a piss."

Ryan chuckled. "I think the health tea will certainly have its drawbacks." He rose from the skeleton he'd searched. "I found bone dust of the undead. Or at least it looks like the bone dust of the undead I saw at the apothecary's shop."

Mallory, who'd searched the other one, held up six arrows. "This is all I found." She glanced at the bone dust. "I wonder what sort of potions it's used for."

Callum took the arrows from her, frowning as he turned towards the fire. "Is our food burning?"

Brodie reached the food first, taking it from the fire. "Probably needs a bit more water in it."

Callum grabbed the waterskin and added water while Mallory stirred it. She peered into the pot. "I think it's ready."

Once they were sitting around the campfire, food served, Smudge eating the last of the fish and Fang more of the bear meat, Mallory opened her character journal. Across the fire from her, Brodie and Callum argued about where they thought the skeletons had come from. She smiled as she went to the new bookmark, wanting to know what type of skills Danae had. Or if she had any.

She was surprised to learn that not only did Danae have a ten percent racial bonus to bow damage, but she also had a racial bonus to mage allowing her to use spells one level above each class level. Danae had one level in unarmed combat that was listed under weapon and armour affinity and under crafting she had level three alchemy, level one bartering, level one cooking and level one glassblowing. She had also unlocked clothier, fishing, languages and scribe, but had no levels in any of them. Danae also had ninety-three points out of one hundred and seven for her next CAS point, which would also give Danae her first character level.

"Danni's stats aren't bad," Ryan said. "Especially since she would have only got her journal a bit over a year ago when she turned fifteen."

Mallory smiled. "I was just checking them."

Ryan grinned. "I started to check them back at the tavern, but I ended up reading some of the notices on the notice board."

Mallory nodded. She looked at him a moment, gathering her thoughts. "Do you think we're doing the right thing? Letting Danni come with us. What if something happens to her?"

"She'll be an archer. She can stay at the back of the group." Ryan handed his empty bowl to Callum, who was collecting them.

Mallory also handed over her bowl. "What are you doing with them?" She nodded to the stack of bowls he carried.

"Brodie is going to walk back into the village with me. We'll fill up the waterskin as well," Callum said.

"We'll leave our companion animals here with you. Both look pretty worn out from the day."

Mallory's gaze was drawn to Smudge and Fang, curled up together, Smudge's paw resting on Fang's snout. A smile formed. "They are so cute together."

"So much for Brodie saying we need a pack animal." Ryan chuckled.

"We couldn't leave her there. Besides, she should be massive when she's full grown. Did you see the size of her mum? Maybe she could wear some kind of saddlebags or pull a small cart." Brodie picked up the waterskin.

Mallory watched Callum and Brodie walk towards the village, the lantern showing the direction they went. "We really need some sort of animal to carry our gear."

"It's going to be a while before we can afford a horse." Ryan added more wood to the fire.

She didn't need to check their coins. She knew exactly how many were left. One gold, twenty-one silver and seventeen copper pieces. And the gold belonged to Smudge. Nowhere near enough to buy a horse. She frowned. "Do you think they have donkeys or mules? Maybe they'd be cheaper than a horse. An animal trained to cart gear rather than be ridden."

Ryan shrugged. "Danni might know." He started to spread out blankets. "We'll have to take turns to keep watch tonight. One at a time should be fine. Especially with Smudge and Fang's hearing." He grinned. "And no drum being played to hide the sounds of anything sneaking up on us."

Smiling, Mallory helped, placing the two thin blankets together and dropping the pillow closer to the fire in the hope it would dry out quicker. By the time the other two returned, they each had one of the thick blankets, an edge pulled over their bodies since the night air was cooler than by the coast.

Brodie looked at the blankets. "Who misses out on somewhere to sleep? It better not be me."

Ryan grinned. "Someone has to keep watch. Sounds like you volunteered to go first."

Brodie glared at them when they laughed. "Our companion animals will let us know if something comes close."

"You're on guard duty," Ryan stated.

Muttering under his breath, Brodie grabbed an apple and sat away from the fire, staring out into the night.

Mallory watched him for a moment, wondering if they should buy more apples before they headed to the mine. They only had one left. She supposed he could eat carrots. There were ten of them. She tried to get more comfortable, pulling the edge of the blanket more firmly over her back, which was away from the fire. "Do you think it snows in this area?"

"We're really going to need to do some grinding to earn money," Ryan said. "Especially if we end up in colder climates."

"And for the XP." She stared into the flames, the warmth of the fire helping her feel sleepy. Before she closed her eyes, she once more checked their journals. If they managed to have eight hours sleep, all of them would have full health before they headed to the mine. But that wouldn't be possible since Ryan needed to take a turn watching. Before she could decide what to do about the matter, she drifted off to sleep, woken hours later by Callum.

"Ryan is on guard duty after you."

She struggled to her feet, tangled in the blanket, the fire still burning. "Okay."

"It helps to keep moving. If you sit down boredom makes you sleepy." Callum straightened out the blanket before lying down.

Chapter Nineteen

Mallory nodded, moving away from the fire. The coolness of the night had her wrapping her arms around herself. She checked everyone's health points. Callum was only down one and Ryan was down four. A smile slowly formed. As bad as losing health points were, at least it was a good way to tell how much time they'd slept. Her smile faded. A pocket watch was yet one more thing they needed. She didn't want to think about how long their list of items, they wanted to buy, was growing.

Pacing around the camp, she slowly warmed up, the coolness of the night keeping her alert. For the next two hours, her attention was caught by every single sound and she wanted to curl up by the fire and go back to sleep. In the end, she decided to take Ryan's watch so he could have full health when they faced the goblins at the mine. She could have a nap in the wagon along the way. Or at least she hoped she could. Who knew what they might encounter along the way. A couple of times she almost changed her mind, worried there wouldn't be time to sleep. Each time she let him sleep, deciding full health was important.

In the early hours of the morning, when it was nearly time to wake the rest of her group, Mallory found a secluded spot behind some shrubs, thinking wistfully of the outhouse in the village. She was gone only minutes, returning to the camp to find Fang playing with the pillow, which had been left by the fire to dry. Clouds of feathers hung in the air, Smudge leaping around batting at them. For a moment she stared at the feathers, mouth gaping. "No!" She grabbed the end of the pillow.

Fang held on, shaking the pillow and trying to drag it from her hands, tail wagging.

"It isn't a game. Let go." Mallory hung onto the pillow, blowing a feather away from her face. Soft laughter drew her attention and she looked over her shoulder to see Ryan getting to his feet.

"Looks like it does snow in this area." Ryan folded his blanket.

"Fang!" Brodie lunged for the wolf cub.

Fang let go of the pillow and jumped out of the

way, barking excitedly. Mallory staggered back, nearly falling over. She looked around the campsite. Smudge caught one of the feathers and held it out to her expectantly. She sighed heavily. "I think we're going to need more than a single feather to salvage this pillow."

Smudge picked up a second feather and held it out too, chirruping.

A smile reluctantly formed and she took the feathers from Smudge and put them back in the pillow. "Thanks."

Ryan glanced around the campsite, taking the pillow from Mallory. "You and Callum see if you can hunt something down for lunch and Brodie can clean up this mess while I cook bear stew for breakfast." He handed the pillow to Brodie.

"Why should I clean it up?" Brodie demanded.

Mallory looked from Fang to the pillow before grabbing her satchel and slipping it over her head and right arm. "Should we take Fang with us?"

"Smudge could stay and help," Callum suggested. "He seems to be good at gathering up the feathers."

After some discussion, it was decided that Mallory and Callum would take Fang and Smudge would stay with Brodie and Ryan, seemingly excited by the prospect of capturing feathers. Mallory started to leave the campsite, but Ryan tugged her back to him.

"What happened to waking me for my turn of keeping watch?" He slid his arms around her waist.

She smiled. "It seemed more logical to make sure we start with full health before we do a fighting quest."

Ryan nodded. "Next time we'll plan it better." His lips brushed across hers before he let go. "Thank you."

She half shrugged. "I can nap on the way to the mine." She glanced at Callum who waited at the edge of the campsite. "I better see what we can find for our lunch before it's time to meet the wagoner."

It took Mallory and Callum about an hour to catch three rabbits, one of them caught by Fang. They returned to the campsite to find breakfast ready, giving the rabbits to Ryan since he was the only one who'd levelled up hunting. It wasn't until they returned to the camp that they realised neither companion animal had earned any experience points while they weren't with their companion.

Brodie told Fang how good she was to catch a rabbit, while Ryan tried to skin and prepare the rabbits. He managed to get meat from two of the rabbits, but no furs from any of them. They gave the carcasses to Fang, who happily settled down by the fire with them. After serving the food in the pot, he put the next lot of stew on. The carrots, potatoes, onion and meat were diced finely so they would cook quicker. He nodded towards the pot as he picked up his bowl. "That's the last of the veggies. I gathered some while you were gone or we wouldn't have had enough for lunch."

"We should be able to collect some on the way to the mine." Mallory smiled when she noticed the pillow had a knot in the corner where Fang had torn it. "Great sewing skills."

Ryan chuckled. "That was your brother's effort. I suggested the needle and thread we got from the cook's assistant."

"It keeps the feathers in." Brodie had a mouthful of food, making a face. "Someone really needs to learn how to cook better. None of our meals taste right." He looked at Mallory. "You've still got a point you haven't used and you want to learn cooking."

"There are other things I need to learn first. Like alchemy." She had a mouthful. "It's a bit tasteless, but isn't too bad. Besides, you've still got a point you haven't used. Why don't you put it into cooking?"

"I wasn't planning to learn how to cook," Brodie said.

Mallory shrugged. "Then I guess you're stuck with crappy food for now."

"Aw, come on, Mal. You don't want to be eating crap for weeks." Brodie absently patted Fang who nudged his bowl.

"It'll be longer than weeks at the rate we're earning XP," Mallory said.

Ryan grinned. "I think Fang is telling you that if you don't want your breakfast she'll have it."

Fang barked once, sitting down beside Brodie, looking up at him.

Brodie fished out a piece of meat from his bowl and gave it to Fang, who licked his fingers clean. "Done. I'm cooking from now on."

Mallory frowned, her expression clearing when she realised what he meant. "You levelled up your cooking?"

Brodie nodded. "You have reached level one cooking. Each level gained allows you to make recipes of that level and you can now use a kitchen knife."

"It'll probably take more than one level to make much of a difference," Callum said.

"We've got that recipe for rich herb gravy." Ryan stirred the pot, handing over the spoon when Brodie held out his hand.

"We need to find the herbs for it." Brodie peered into the pot. "Do you think the herbs will be enough to help with the taste without beef stock and flour?"

"Flour will be to thicken it," Mallory said. "They would use stock instead of water to add to the flavour of the gravy. You'd think the herbs would help though."

Once they'd eaten, Mallory, Callum and Smudge walked to the village taking the dishes with them in the basket along with the spare bow. Ryan, Brodie and Fang remained to pack up the camp and finish cooking. They organised to meet out the front of the blacksmith shop, which was on the road out of Wayholt.

Mallory and Callum cleaned off the dishes at the well then headed to the tavern where they found the wagoner seated at a table, having his breakfast, Danae sitting with him. The wagoner gave them a nod in greeting, having had a mouthful of food.

Danae rose, grinning when she saw them, bending to pat Smudge when they came close. "Are we ready to go? I only need to collect my horse and then I'm ready." A satchel sat on the floor beside her seat, looking rather full, and she was dressed in black trousers and a dark red blouse that was edged with embroidery, a belt with a belt pouch sitting low on her hips.

Chapter Twenty

Mallory sat the basket on the edge of the table. "We're waiting for Ryan to pack up camp and Brodie to finish cooking a rabbit stew for lunch."

Danae gestured towards her satchel. "I brought food."

"We'll be gone overnight. That doesn't look like you have enough food to last that long." Callum held out the bow and half a dozen arrows. "Stick beside me when we're fighting so you can grab more arrows. We don't have a spare quiver."

Danae glanced at her satchel. "Beef and vegetable pasties mightn't be overly large, but they're filling." She took the bow and arrows. "I've got a bit of gold from helping my father in his shop. I'll see if one of the shops here has a quiver for sale." Danae picked up her satchel and slung it into place along with her bow. "Shall I meet you out the front of the blacksmith shop too? I've also got to collect my horse from the stables."

"We'd like to visit the stables." Callum scooped up Smudge from where he leaned against his leg. He turned to the wagoner, who was still eating. "We'll meet you outside the blacksmith shop when you're done."

"That sounds fine. I'll be ready in about fifteen minutes," the wagoner said.

Danae led the way to the secondhand shop where she was able to buy a quiver. Afterwards, she cut across the village to the stables, which were out the back of the trading post.

While Danae collected her horse, Mallory looked at the listing of animals for sale on the noticeboard inside the stables. She stared at the prices, slowly shaking her head. Seventy-five gold pieces for a horse was going to take a long time to earn. Even eight gold pieces for a mule was out of their reach.

"So much for getting better gear and equipment this time," Callum said softly.

"Maybe they'll pay us well for getting rid of the goblins," Mallory suggested.

"Do you really believe that?"

She sighed heavily. "Not really." She headed outside to wait for Danae, Callum walking at her side.

"There have to be better ways to level up and earn money."

Callum shrugged. "Danni might know since she's grown up in this world."

Danae came out of the stables leading a saddled bay Andalusian mare. Her reddish-brown coat gleamed and her black mane and tail were braided with dark red ribbons that matched Danae's blouse. "Meet Augusta." She smiled. "I named her after those pretty white flowers that have a stronger scent of an evening. I was about five or six at the time when my father bought her and I convinced him to let me come up with a name." She patted the horse. "But I think the name suits her. The flowers are used in stamina potions and she certainly has plenty of that."

Mallory's gaze was drawn to the saddlebags. "I can't wait until we can afford horses."

Danae walked beside them. "Here. You might as well have this now. Health tea, like I promised. And the recipe." She handed a full waterskin to Mallory along with a folded piece of paper. She nodded towards her horse. "They make it quicker to go places. Not that I get to go many places since it isn't good to travel alone. Each time my father came home, back when he was a peddler, he told some of the most interesting stories. I always begged him to take me along, but he'd say it was too dangerous. I've hardly been anywhere." A smile momentarily appeared. "I can't wait until I travel to Eridell to attend the Alchemy Academy. That will be the furthest I've ever travelled."

"How far away is Eridell?" Callum asked.

"Depending which part of Eridell you wish to visit. Merrow, the town I'm going to is about fifty-four nautical miles away by ship. The Green Isles aren't far off the coast and you can see the mainland from the eastern side of Ruby Isle. Just like you can see Opal Isle from the northern end of Ruby Isle," Danae said.

"How long does that take by ship?" Callum asked.

"A ship can reach Merrow in as little as nine hours if there's a mage onboard who can do weather spells. Longer if they don't and the winds aren't cooperating," Danae said.

"Nine hours isn't long," Mallory said. She'd expected it to be longer than that.

"Does that mean you'll visit me while I'm living in Eridell?" Danae asked.

"We're planning on moving to the mainland eventually." Mallory smiled when she saw Ryan walking towards her, the wagoner sitting on his wagon outside the blacksmith shop and Brodie hurrying after Ryan with Fang at his heels.

"You are?" Danae asked.

"We are what?" Ryan asked.

"Moving to Eridell," Callum said. "Eventually."

Danae smiled in greeting, her gaze going from Ryan to Brodie. "I brought beef and vegetable pasties with me."

"Cool." Brodie fell into step with Danae as they continued walking towards the wagon.

Danae glanced around the group. "You might want to look at the area around Merrow. It's a reasonable sized port town and has a couple of other academies there as well as a few guilds and a lot of different shops and tradesmen."

"Sounds good." Brodie turned to Mallory. "Don't you think?"

Reaching the wagon, Callum put Smudge down between the chests before climbing up to join him. "We also need an area with plenty of resources."

"There are farmlands in one direction from the town, but in the other direction it's fairly untouched so there are plenty of resources. A lot don't travel in that direction because of the ruins several hours away." Danae swung into the saddle.

"Ruins sound interesting." Ryan sat on the end of the wagon once Mallory was in, Brodie sitting beside him.

Mallory moved the pot of food out of the way and took the blanket Ryan held out to her. "Ruins sound dangerous."

Danae rode alongside the wagon. "Oh, they are. All sorts of creatures come out of the depths of the ruins. The perfect area for adventurers."

Mallory made herself comfortable. "That probably depends on how high a level the creatures in the ruins are compared to the adventurers going there."

Ryan chuckled, looking over his shoulder at Mallory. "Something for us to look forward to?"

Mallory smiled. "If it was an actual RPG I'd head to the nearest town and steal everything not nailed down and sell it to fund my early game. But I think the guardians would frown on that."

"They don't mind if you do that in the dark forces settlements," Danae said.

Mallory sat up, her mouth open as she tried to come up with words. "What?"

"I said that–"

Mallory interrupted Danae. "No, I heard what you said. I just don't understand what you mean by the dark forces settlements."

"They have to live somewhere, don't they?" Danae asked.

Mallory tried to speak several times. Ryan spoke before she could come up with a coherent reply.

"What's the catch?"

"They come after you if you target them."

"Makes sense," Ryan said.

"We going to raid a dark forces settlement?" Brodie asked. "Not like we haven't already attacked some of them." He glanced at Fang. "And I'd do it again."

"I don't know." Mallory's gaze was unfocused as she thought of the possibilities and potential problems. "There's also that sunken ship we want to look into. The one with the enchanted staff. And there's Bard's Hollow to explore."

"I wonder if there'll be skeletons in the cave like the ones that attacked us last night," Brodie said.

The wagoner looked over his shoulder. "You were attacked by skeletons?"

Mallory nodded. "Two of them. Archers."

"There must be an ancient crypt in the area. I wonder what's causing the skeletons to spawn. Someone is probably going to need to find out what triggered them to spawn and sort it out before it becomes a problem for Wayholt," the wagoner said.

Mallory laughed softly when she noticed the journal icon appear and saw there was a new quest. *Ancient Crypt: Discover the ancient crypt near Wayholt and learn why skeletons are wandering the area before the undead have the chance to descend upon the village.*

"What's with all the quests?" Brodie demanded.

Ryan chuckled. "Don't talk to people and we won't gain any."

"As if that's possible," Brodie muttered.

"That quest sounds like a lot of fun," Danae said.

Brodie looked towards the half-elf. "Fun?" He sounded uncertain.

Chapter Twenty-One

Mallory barely managed to hide a smile. "It might be too tough for us."

"There are five of us for now," Danae said.

"I do need to reach Surith before too much longer," the wagoner said.

"We can always come back this way," Ryan said.

Mallory got comfortable again. "I suppose so."

Danae sighed heavily. "I would have really liked to go on that quest."

"You don't have to go straight home, do you?" Brodie asked. "There's time before you have to turn up at your academy."

Danae's expression brightened momentarily. "No, I should go there as soon as I can. There are always hold ups along the way. Look at how my journey was originally postponed."

Mallory's eyes closed as the conversation between

Danae and Brodie drifted over her. A paw patted her cheek and she half opened her eyes to see Smudge watching over her. Smiling, she closed her eyes and drifted off to sleep, tired after her four-hour watch during the night.

She was jarred awake, the wagon on an angle and the road rough. Above her towered a sheer cliff and she struggled to sit up so she could see where they were. "How far away are we?" A blanket pooled around her waist and she guessed it had been placed over her while she slept.

The wagoner drew out his pocket watch. "About fifteen minutes from the mine. We left the main road a bit ago and this is the road that leads to the mine."

Sitting up straighter she looked around. There were a few pine trees and the cliff was only on their left, a sloping mountainside on the right. The road was wide enough that two carts could easily pass each other, ruts in the road causing the wagon to regularly jolt as they travelled up the steep incline. There were a handful of herbs along the side of the road amongst scattered clumps of grass.

"You aren't going to pick any herbs, Danni?" Mallory looked from the herbs to the half-elf who continued to ride alongside the cart.

"Brodie and Ryan helped me pick some earlier.

I don't want to overfill my saddlebags. I'll see how much space I have on the way back before I gather more," Danae said. "Brodie wanted to even up the XP in the group." She smiled. "But I think it will take a while for him to catch up to my level."

Chuckling, Ryan held out a spoon to Mallory. "The last of the stew, in the pot, is yours. The wagoner said it should last a while in this weather."

"I offered to eat it in case it didn't, but Ryan wouldn't let me." Brodie sent another glare towards Ryan, having already given him one for laughing at Danae's comment.

"Why doesn't that surprise me?" Mallory drew the pot onto her lap, smiling when Fang and Smudge moved closer, both staring wistfully at her. Sighing, she fished out a piece of meat for each of them. They were impossible to resist.

"I need to learn how to make those expressions." Brodie gestured towards the companion animals.

Ryan chuckled. "Spare us. I don't think we could survive your attempts."

Mallory ate the stew, smiling at the good-natured arguing between Brodie and Ryan, Callum joining them. She hated to admit it, but this meal was slightly better than the previous ones they'd cooked. It looked like Brodie's single cooking level had made a difference. Finished eating, she looked around. "What are we going to do about cleaning the dirty dishes?"

Ryan took the pot from her and added it to the bowls in the basket. "The wagoner said there'll be a well at the mine. We can clean everything there."

Ahead was a palisade across the road and the wagoner slowed as they approached, two guards standing on either side of the open gate. Mallory couldn't take her gaze off the large guards. They reminded her of Grotmur Blackhelm, but their skin was a different colour. "What are they?"

"Orcs," Danae said.

They had grey skin, bulging arm muscles, protruding lower canines, were about six and a half feet tall and carried spears. They were dressed in leather trousers and boots and wore hide vests.

"The orc we met in Wayholt was a greenish grey," Callum said.

"Some are a greenish grey and some are a darker grey like charcoal while others are the same stone grey colour as these two," Danae said.

They fell silent as the wagoner drew to a halt.

One of the orcs came forward. "What's your business?"

"I wish to see the overseer about purchasing ore

and those travelling with me have come about the goblin problem," the wagoner said.

The orc eyed them up and down. "You lot are going to take care of the goblins?" When they nodded, he glanced at his fellow guard, both of them laughing. The orc stepped back, still grinning. "Go on in. Leave your wagon over beside the overseer's building on the right. You can't miss it. Fanciest building we've got."

The wagoner nodded. "Thank you." He urged his horses forward.

The moment they pulled up beside the only stone building, Ryan hopped off the back of the wagon, taking the basket of dirty dishes with him. "I'll wash these if someone wants to talk to the overseer."

"Do you need a hand?" Mallory asked even though she really wanted to hear what the overseer had to say.

Ryan grinned. "Go talk to the overseer. I've got this."

She returned his grin. "Thanks." Glancing around the area, she saw a mine entrance at the back in the middle of the clearing, a long timber building and two smaller timber buildings off to the left as well as the stone building on the right, which they'd parked beside. A man came towards them from the stone building. He might not have been as tall as the orcs, but he was as solidly built as both of them and carried a pick at his side where a sword would usually hang.

The overseer stopped in front of the wagoner, shaking his hand. "Trader, I take it?"

"Of a fashion. Mostly I transport and sell goods for people and take a percentage of the sale on their behalf. Today I'm looking to buy ore to trade in Surith."

The overseer looked towards Mallory and her party, other than Ryan, who had joined her. "Your assistants?"

Mallory shook her head. "We came to deal with the goblin problem and deliver a letter to Kruth Blackhelm from his brother." She nearly asked why the orcs couldn't deal with the goblins, but decided that wasn't the way to be given the quest. Maybe there weren't enough guards to protect the mine and take care of the goblins too.

The overseer cleared his throat several times. "You sure you're up to dealing with the goblins? Two of our guards went in and we haven't seen them since. We can't spare any more, not that orcs are that great against goblins. Cunning little devils they are. Orcs might be strong, but they aren't the quickest of thinkers."

"You only have orcs for guards?" Callum asked.

The overseer spread his hands expansively. "They're tough fighters and look impressive. Can use weapons ten levels above their class level. None of the humans were willing to go in with the orcs. Not that there are many of us here. Most of the miners are dwarves. They're as good as born with the ability to sniff out ores."

"What class and level are the orcs that went missing?" Danae asked.

"Warrior level one," the overseer said.

Ryan joined them in time to hear Danae's question. "Better yet, who are the orcs that went missing?"

"It's not Kruth Blackhelm, is it?" Mallory asked.

"I'm afraid so." Again the overseer spread his hands expansively. "He volunteered. Was interested in the reward. Him and the other guard. All they had to do was get rid of the goblins in the mine tunnel and find out how they got into the tunnel and I'd give them five gold pieces."

"Where is the tunnel?" Brodie asked.

Chapter Twenty-Two

Mallory grinned at her brother's enthusiasm, sobering before she spoke to the overseer. "We won't be able to deal with the goblins and get back to Wayholt before dark. Is there somewhere we can set up camp for the night?"

The overseer gestured towards the space next to the stone building where the wagon was. "Plenty of space for you there."

Mallory was tempted to disagree. There was probably five metres between the building and the steep side of the mountain. An almost vertical wall of rock for at least ten metres high with jagged, rough sections the rest of the way to the summit.

"How are we all meant to fit there?" Brodie asked.

The overseer once more spread his hands expansively as he spoke. "Others manage without a problem. Grateful not to be out in the wilds with the bandits and bears."

"It's okay-" Mallory broke off at the shouts coming from the mine entrance. As she watched, a group of dwarves and humans came out of the mine, four of them carting a metal cage that was approximately half a metre square while the other three carried timber buckets of water. Her gaze was fixed on the creature in the cage.

The red creature was rather draconic looking with its leathery wings, body like a frilled necked lizard without the frill and scaly skin. Every time it tried to open its mouth and spread its wings one of the humans tossed half a bucket of water at it. The bucket was half filled again by one of the other two carrying buckets and the human went back to watching the creature.

"What is that?" Callum asked.

"You're not getting one," Brodie stated.

The overseer chuckled. "You certainly wouldn't want one around that age. It's a fire drake. You can also get frost and poison ones too. The best time to get them is either when they're about to hatch or just hatched. Only hatchlings are trainable." He nodded towards the fire drake having another bucket of water tossed in its face. "One that age can't be taught much at all. Too feral."

"Then why did you capture it?" Ryan asked.

"Made a nest for itself in one of the tunnels. What else could I do?" The overseer spread his hands expansively. "I'll sell it to one of the breeders over near Shadhurst. I'll make a tidy profit on it and they'll make a nice profit on the hatchlings."

"How much is a hatchling worth? Mallory asked.

"You're not getting one either," Brodie stated. "Why can't anyone remember we need a pack animal?"

The overseer shrugged. "Depends on the bloodlines. You could pay as little as a hundred gold pieces or as much as a thousand."

"As little?"

Mallory smiled at the disbelieving tone her brother used. It echoed her thoughts.

"How will you stop it from setting the place on fire?" Ryan asked. "Or transport it to Shadhurst."

"We'll stack ores around it." The overseer gestured towards the mine. "You still interested in dealing with those goblins?"

Mallory glanced around her group. Danae and Ryan grinned, Callum shrugged and Brodie nodded.

She faced the overseer again. "We'll take care of the goblins in the mine and find out how they got in."

The overseer beckoned over one of the dwarven miners. The rest of the miners were stacking ore around the cage of the fire drake. "Show these adventurers to the blocked off tunnel and let them in. Make sure you block it up again and wait for them to return."

"You're locking us in there?" Brodie demanded.

Mallory had been about to ask the same question.

The overseer spread his hands again. "You don't expect us to leave it open and risk our lives do you?"

"I'll wait by the entrance as long as necessary," the dwarf said. "You can count on me. I'd also really appreciate it if you keep a watch out for Kruth. He's a good friend. Didn't seem right not to go after him. But I'm only a miner, not a warrior." The dwarf was shorter than Mallory, only five feet tall and had a thick brown beard that went past his leather belt. As he said the word 'miner' he touched the pick hanging at his side.

Mallory nodded. "His brother is worried about him and asked us to personally deliver a letter to him."

The dwarf smiled, his expression mostly hidden by his beard. "That's a relief." He glanced over his shoulder towards the long timber building. "I'll grab myself some food in case you're in the tunnel for a while."

"We'll wait for you by the mine entrance," Ryan said.

The overseer turned to the wagoner. "You want to join me inside where we can discuss trade prices and items?"

Callum held out a hand, as if to stop the wagoner. "Wait a minute. Do we still have the use of one of the chests?"

The wagoner nodded. "Until we return to Buckneth."

"Thanks," Callum said.

"No, I am the one who should be thanking you. It's always a more profitable trip travelling to Wayholt, but it's rare I have the opportunity." With a nod towards them, the wagoner followed the overseer inside the stone building.

"We'll leave most of our gear in the chest in case the goblins have some good drops." Ryan strode to the wagon and sat the backpack on the edge as he removed most of the contents and put them in the chest they'd used earlier.

While he sorted out the backpack, Mallory checked the journal icon in the corner of her vision. As she'd expected, it was for discovering the mine. But instead of the usual ten experience points, this time they'd gained fifteen. It might be worth visiting more mines for the extra experience points. She also checked the updated quests, reading them over to herself.

Unwanted Residents: Get rid of the goblins in the mine tunnel and find out how they got in to receive five gold pieces.

Missing Guard: Discover why Kruth never returned from the goblin tunnel in South Peak Mine.

There was no unexpected information or hints as to what they could expect. Checking over everyone else's journals, before they went into the mine, she discovered Danae had levelled up her character. "Are you going to sort out your level up, Danni? You have five attribute points you can use."

"I wasn't sure if you wanted me to come on more adventures with you. I wouldn't be able to join you all the time, but the workload at the Alchemy Academy isn't meant to be overly heavy. If you're based in the area I could come along on some of your adventures and quests," Danae said.

Brodie spoke before Mallory could open her mouth. "Hell yeah. You can come with us any time."

Ryan looked up from the backpack, chuckling. "Not being party leader doesn't seem to have caused much of a problem for you."

When both Mallory and Callum laughed, Danae looked uncertain. "You don't want me to join you on future adventures?"

Still smiling, Mallory shook her head. "That wasn't what we were laughing at. Like Brodie said, you're welcome to join us any time."

Danae's expression cleared and she smiled. "Thank you. I can help you with some of the crafting abilities I know. Like the alchemy ingredients I'll learn about at the academy."

"How about teaching us your languages crafting ability?" Brodie asked.

"That's easy enough. All I need to do is teach you a word in Elvish to unlock it," Danae said.

"We should leave that for later," Callum said. "We don't want the miner waiting all afternoon for us."

"I'll put one of my attribute points in strength. It's always good to be able to carry a bit more and I'll put two each in constitution and dexterity. The first for the extra health and the second because it's an archer attribute."

"Hey, you've got a revive now," Brodie said.

Danae nodded. "Yes, I gained it when I levelled up."

"I really need to level up so I can get another revive," Brodie said.

"I hope it doesn't take a year like it did for Danni," Callum said. "Do you gain your character journal at the start of your birthday?"

"It goes on the hour of birth. Luckily I was born in the early hours of the morning so didn't have to wait all day and night for my journal to form. And it won't take you as long as it took me to reach character level one. Adventurers earn XP quicker than those who focus on their crafting abilities." Danae smiled. "I'm finished distributing my points and levelling up my class." She paused a moment. "You have reached level one archer. You can now wield slings and use sling ammunition."

Chapter Twenty-Three

"Are slings useful?" Mallory asked.

Danae nodded. "You can nearly always find pebbles to use in them and ammunition is a lot cheaper than it is for a bow if you want to buy some of the other types of ammunition such as lead. They make a good back up for long journeys."

Ryan lit the lantern, the backpack already in place. "Let's see what we can do about the goblin problem." He left his shield on the back of the wagon, leaning it against the chest beside the fishing pole.

Callum scooped up Smudge while Fang trotted at Brodie's heel.

The miner was waiting for them at the entrance. He wore a mining helmet with a lantern in it and also carried a lit lantern. He gestured to the one Ryan carried. "I wasn't sure you'd have one. But a bit more light won't go astray."

Mallory took the lantern from the miner. "How far into the mine is the tunnel?"

"Not far. A few minutes walk." The dwarf led the way.

Callum continued to carry Smudge while Fang walked at Brodie's side. Mallory took one last look at the sky before she entered the dark mine behind Ryan and Danae. A shiver went through her. Although the tunnel was wider than she expected, it was going to be cramped when it came to fighting. Exactly how clever were goblins? She supposed she'd soon find out.

The miner led them through a maze of tunnels stopping at one with large boulders piled in front of it. He rolled several boulders out of the way and stepped back. "Here we are. You call out to me when you return and I'll hear you."

Mallory entered last, the wand in one hand and the lantern in the other. Could goblins see in the dark? She turned back to ask, but the miner had already rolled the boulders back into place. She supposed he could hear her, but she'd wanted to also see his expression to get a better idea of what they were in for. She moved closer to the boulder. "Can you hear me?"

"I sure can," the miner said.

"Can goblins see in the dark?"

"Didn't think about that," Ryan said.

"Not exactly see in the dark. They don't need much light to be able to see their surroundings," the miner said.

"Okay, thanks." Mallory faced the rest of the group. "We ready?"

"I badly need some XP so I can level up and get a revive again," Brodie said.

"Sounds good to me. I wouldn't mind unlocking one of the other classes so I can use a ranged weapon at the start of some fights." Ryan led the way further into the tunnel.

"Why don't you level up hunting so you can use a hunting bow?" Danae asked.

"I didn't know it was a possibility. What is a hunting bow like and at what level do you unlock it?" Ryan asked.

"About half the attack of a short bow, but at higher levels you can use an enchanted one. You have the ability to use one at level five hunting," Danae said.

Smudge, who was still in Callum's arms, made several soft, high-pitched sounds.

Callum put him on the ground. "I think there's something ahead." He kept his voice low.

"I think there is too because Fang is growling softly." Brodie drew out two of his throwing knives.

"I can't see very far ahead." Mallory thought longingly of spotlights and powerful modern torches.

"You can get a magelight spell when you're a higher level," Danae suggested.

Mallory didn't have the chance to ask anything about spells or mage levels. Three goblins came running out of the darkness at them, clubs raised. They were four feet tall, dark green, wore ragged clothes and their open mouths showed sharp teeth. She automatically threw fireballs at two of them, Danae taking out the third one before she could attack it and Brodie finishing off one goblin while Ryan finished off the other. She stared at the bodies, dazed that the fight had ended before it had begun.

"That's it?" Brodie asked.

"I didn't get a chance to attack anything," Callum said.

Brodie grinned. "We should go after more goblins."

"No wonder the mercenaries weren't interested in this quest," Ryan said.

"They must only have seven health at the most," Callum said. "Since that's Danni's crit attack."

"Then I obviously didn't do a crit attack on them," Mallory said. "Because my crit is eight."

"We should search the bodies and keep going." Ryan crouched beside one of the goblins. "We have to figure out how they're getting in."

A search gave them two copper coins, a pair of goblin boots and a chisel. Mallory stared at the boots. "What are we meant to do with these?"

"They're small enough a kid could wear them," Callum said.

"You can sell them to a shop. Someone will buy them for their child," Danae said.

"We should find more goblins to kill. That was an easy three XP," Brodie said.

"As long as you don't get goblin hordes." Callum scooped up Smudge, who he'd set down while using his bow.

Brodie turned to Danae. "Do you?"

"I don't know if they can be called a horde. Some goblins live in settlements."

"Start moving," Ryan said.

Brodie followed Ryan, remaining at Danae's side. "How big is a goblin settlement?"

"From about twenty to fifty goblins."

Mallory stared at Danae's back, tempted to ask if she'd heard right. Fifty goblins? A handful wasn't so bad, but that many would be too much for them to survive. "If we come across fifty goblins, run back to the entrance."

Mallory had barely finished speaking when a group of goblins ran towards them. Five of them were the same height as the earlier ones they'd faced, one was a couple of inches taller than the rest of the group. Mallory attacked the taller one, as did Ryan. When the goblin fell, she attacked another. Ryan turned to the last goblin standing, taking him out with Callum's help.

"That wasn't as bad as I thought it would be." Brodie knelt beside one of the bodies, searching it.

"I was a bit worried about this one." Ryan searched the tallest goblin, his lantern on the ground beside him.

Danae handed a copper coin to Mallory, finished searching a goblin. "He would have been a goblin leader. The only difference between him and the other goblins is that he has more health. And is a little taller. It's the goblin generals you have to watch out for. They're about half a foot taller and have double the stats. You usually find them in settlements."

By the time they finished searching the bodies of the goblins, they'd found two copper pieces, another chisel and a hundred grams of jerky. Mallory eyed the jerky. "Is this edible for humans?"

Danae smiled. "They don't make jerky. Stew is about as good as their culinary expertise reaches. They tend to eat a lot of raw food. Even raw meat." She gestured towards the jerky. "They probably stole this from a miner. Or some unsuspecting traveller."

Brodie took the jerky. "I'll have it." He slipped it into his belt pouch.

Mallory started to disagree then changed her mind. She didn't care how edible it was. None of the goblins had looked very clean to her.

"Are you ready to keep going?" Ryan nodded in the direction they'd been heading, both hands full. Sword in one hand, the lantern in the other.

"I am," Brodie said. "We need to find more goblins. This XP is awesome."

It didn't take long to reach the end of the tunnel and find a narrow opening with a bit of rubble scattered on the ground. Ryan peered inside the opening, holding his lantern in first. "The majority of the rubble is inside the dungeon. I'd say miners broke through just enough for the goblins to discover this tunnel."

"Dungeon?" Mallory tugged Ryan out of the way, putting the lantern inside the hole before she had a look. There was a pile of rubble near the opening, covering part of a cracked, paved floor. The room was approximately three metres long and two metres wide. To the left and right were closed wooden doors, the aged timber looking like it had been there for a century. Or possibly longer. Apart from the rubble, and a scattering of dirt across the floor, the room was empty. A shiver of anticipation raced through her. A dungeon. An actual dungeon.

"Hurry up. I want to have a look." Brodie tugged on Mallory's arm.

"I earned XP for finding a location," Ryan said.

Chapter Twenty-Four

Mallory moved back, letting Brodie take the lantern before she checked her journal. Her mouth momentarily hung open. "Twenty XP for discovering a dungeon. We need to find more of them."

"I told you adventurers level up quickly," Danae said. "Travelling to the capital will give you the best XP for a location." She took the lantern from Brodie and checked inside the opening of the dungeon, stepping out of the way and handing the lantern over to Callum so he could have a look.

"What if we get lost in there?" Callum asked.

Ryan shook his head. "We shouldn't do. We've got a compass."

"I was wondering what we had that for. We've never really used it," Brodie said.

While they talked Mallory checked her journal and

everyone else's. "We really need to do more adventuring. Have you checked your stats? Look at how much XP we've earned since we arrived at the mine. All of us except for Danae earned another CAS point. We're halfway to our first character level."

"Hell yeah!" Brodie victory punched the air. "Let's find more goblins."

Ryan chuckled. "We should let the overseer know what we learned. If we're lucky, it will finish one quest and start another."

"And if we're not lucky?" Brodie asked.

"There'll be another stage to the quest." Ryan took a step away from the opening. "But I'm betting it will be the end of this quest because all he said was to deal with the goblins in the tunnel and find out how they got in."

Mallory rechecked the wording of the quest. *Unwanted Residents: Get rid of the goblins in the mine tunnel and find out how they got in to receive five gold pieces.* Ryan was right. They'd dealt with the ones in the tunnel and they'd learned how they'd managed to get in. "Okay, let's see if we can trigger a second quest for a bit more XP."

"And another reward," Brodie said.

It didn't take long to return to the blocked

entrance. Ryan stood close to the boulders. "You still there?"

The dwarf answered instantly. "I certainly am. How you doing in there?"

Mallory moved closer to the boulders. "We're ready to come out. We know how the goblins are getting in."

The dwarf moved some boulders out of the way. "Did you find the guards?"

Mallory stepped past the boulders before she spoke. "Not yet. We thought we should let the overseer know what's happening." For a moment she worried that returning to the overseer might risk the lives of the missing guards. But surely the small amount of time it'd take to talk to him wouldn't make that much of a difference.

Ryan was the last one out of the goblin tunnel. "You'll need to put those boulders back in place. We cleaned out the tunnel, but they can still get in."

"Where are they coming from?" The dwarf pushed the boulders back into place.

"Whoever was mining in that tunnel broke into a dungeon. They might not have noticed because most of the rubble is in the dungeon from the goblins breaking into the tunnel." Ryan strode beside the dwarf, who led the way through the maze of tunnels.

Mallory tried to remember the path out of the mine, but it was impossible. There were too many different tunnels. She had a feeling the dwarf led them through side tunnels rather than along main ones. "Do you know where the overseer will be?" Mallory asked as they stepped outside.

The dwarf gestured towards the stone building. "He'll be in there. Want me to get him for you?"

Ryan nodded. "Thanks." He followed the miner who strode towards the stone building.

They waited out the front of the stone building, Brodie chewing on some of his jerky. "We need to find ways to store food." He glanced to where the fire drake was hidden by a pile of ore. "Do you think a frost drake would work? You know, like a kind of fridge to keep things cold."

"What you need is an enchanted chest or box," Danae said.

"Enchanted?" Brodie asked.

"Yes. Enchanted to keep things cold."

Brodie's expression of confusion cleared. "How do you get one of them?"

"A chest doesn't sound like something easy to cart around." Mallory's gaze was momentarily drawn to the chests on the wagon that the horses were no longer hitched to.

"They aren't," Danae said. "They're something you'd store in a house or tavern. Although I hear the travellers sometimes have them in their caravans."

"We really need to set up a base," Callum said.

"That won't help us while we're travelling." Ryan put out the lantern.

Mallory put hers out too. "Can you get them in a small box?"

"Yes, but they're expensive," Danae said.

"What are travellers?" Brodie asked.

"They travel around in their caravans. You won't see them on an island. Not enough trade opportunities for them. They live their entire lives in their caravans, along with their family." Danae smiled. "Can you imagine the places they must see and the stories they'd have to tell?"

"They're like peddlers?" Callum asked.

Danae shook her head. "They're a faction of travelling clans. Some groups buy and trade items, others are entertainers and some are craftsmen. Some are a mixture. You never know what you might discover when travellers come to a place. My father told me about them. It's why he moved to Ruby Isle instead of being a peddler in Eridell."

Before Mallory had a chance to ask any questions, the overseer came outside, followed by the wagoner.

She went forward to talk to him. "We found out how the goblins got into the mine tunnel and we got rid of the ones that were currently in the tunnel. There were nine and they came from a dungeon."

Ryan spoke when Mallory stopped. "We think one of your miners weakened the wall of the dungeon enough that the goblins noticed and broke through, but not enough that the miner would have noticed."

The overseer turned to the dwarf. "Find out who were the last two working in that tunnel."

The dwarf nodded, heading back into the mine.

"They aren't going to get into trouble, are they?" Mallory asked. "Most of the rubble was on the dungeon side, not the tunnel side."

"That will depend on what they tell me." The overseer took five gold coins out of his belt pouch, holding them out to Mallory. "As agreed upon. I don't suppose you're interested in cleaning out the dungeon. We don't need a goblin settlement around here. All it will take is killing the goblin general and the rest of them will go looking for a new general to follow."

Mallory slipped the coins into a pocket. "Thanks. We'll discuss it and let you know."

The wagoner took a step towards them. "I'd like to leave early enough tomorrow morning to reach

Wayholt before dark." He held up a pocket watch. The winding key was attached by a chain and it had a metal cover to protect the face. He opened it to display the face of the watch, the time almost three. "You can borrow my pocket watch so you're back in time to leave. I'll wind it if you wish to use it so you don't have to worry about it stopping before it's time to return. Shall we plan to leave at eight tomorrow morning?"

"No need to leave so soon." The overseer spread his hands expansively. "I don't mind if you want to stay another night. You can join us for the evening meal."

Mallory glanced at Brodie, worried he might accept. She grinned when she noticed Callum had elbowed her brother. "We need to discuss it."

"The pocket watch runs a little fast, but it was reset using the time of a larger clock within the past week so it's pretty much on time." The wagoner slipped it back into his pocket. "Let me know if you wish to borrow it."

The overseer took a step closer to them, standing beside the wagoner. "I'll pay you another five gold if you bring me the short sword wielded by their general. It will have their clan symbol engraved on the blade. Usually some type of animal."

"Give us a couple of minutes to talk it over."

Mallory strode to the wagon, worried her brother might say something with both food and gold on offer. The rest of the group followed. Before she had the chance to say anything, Brodie spoke.

"Are you crazy? Five gold pieces. That would give us ten for the day. And dinner."

Chapter Twenty-Five

Ignoring her brother, Mallory turned to Danae. "Did you want one-fifth of what we earn?"

"No, not with all you've given me." Danae glanced at the bow she held. "And letting me join your party." She grinned. "I'll take a share from future adventures."

"Okay. That sounds fair enough." Before Mallory could ask Danae if she was interested in doing the quest, Brodie interrupted her.

"What about the quest?"

"I was getting to that," Mallory said. "Let me check the details first to make sure there aren't any surprises." She opened the journal and read the updated and new quest aloud. "Unwanted Residents: After clearing the tunnel of goblins and discovering how they entered you were rewarded with five gold pieces for your party. You also earned fifteen experience points each. Unwanted Residents Part

Two: The overseer has offered five gold pieces for the death of the goblin general and his sword as proof."

Ryan chuckled. "Part two. I wouldn't mind doing the quest. If we come across twenty or more goblins we can always run."

"Three votes," Callum said.

Danae frowned, looking at each of them. "What do three votes mean?"

"We vote on whether or not we do things." Ryan grinned. "Majority rules."

"Does that mean I have no choice but to join you on the quest?" Danae asked.

"No," Mallory said. "Since we're somewhere safe, you can stay behind if you want."

Danae shook her head. "I want to go. I was curious as to how things work in your party."

"I can tell the overseer we'll do the quest?" Brodie glanced over his shoulder to the overseer who remained out the front of the stone building.

"We should have something to eat first," Callum said. "We don't want to have to worry about stopping for food in the dungeon. That doesn't sound like a good plan."

"I've got beef and vegetable pasties." Danae's hand rested against her satchel.

"Okay. Food and then we go," Brodie said.

Mallory glanced at Ryan, smiling when she saw his grin. She nodded. "Food and then we do the quest." She made her tone serious, her gaze going to her brother. "But if we're outnumbered, we run."

"I'm not about to stick around when I have no revive." Brodie took the pastie Danae handed him, biting into the golden pastry after he thanked her.

After having two beef and vegetable pasties each, also sharing some with the companion animals, and putting the chisels and boots in the chest, they returned to the overseer. The dwarf, who'd led them to the tunnel earlier, stood beside him. "Did you come to a decision?" The overseer spread his hands. "You interested in taking my offer?"

Mallory looked from the dwarf to the overseer. "What happened to the miners who were last working in the blocked off tunnel?"

"From what you said and what they told me, I decided it was an accident." The overseer spread his hands, this time shrugging as well. "One of the hazards of being a miner." He looked at each of them. "Your decision?"

"We'll see what we can do," Mallory said.

At the same time, Brodie said, "We'll do the quest. Do we still get dinner even if we don't need to stay two nights?"

The overseer chuckled. "If you bring me the sword of the goblin general before dinner is done, not only will I give you a meal but an extra gold piece as well."

"Hell yeah," Brodie said. "We'll see you for dinner."

"What time is dinner?" Callum asked.

"Seven thirty. It's usually over by eight," the overseer said.

"I'll see you then." Brodie strode towards the mine entrance.

Mallory glanced between her brother and the overseer. "Will you be sending a miner with us again? I doubt we could find the tunnel without help."

Before the overseer could speak, the dwarf did. "It would be an honour to guide you again." He waited for Ryan to take the pocket watch the wagoner held out before he led the way to the mine entrance. He paused by the entrance to fill the lanterns and his helmet with oil, lighting each of them. "You all ready?"

"Yeah, let's go," Brodie said.

Mallory checked the update for the quest, smiling when she read it to herself. *Unwanted Residents Part Two: The overseer challenged you to finish before the evening meal ends and he will both feed you and pay an extra gold coin.* Noticing the dwarf looked in her direction, she nodded in answer to his question.

Once again the dwarf led them through the tunnels to the one that was blocked off. He pushed several boulders out of the way and stepped back. "I brought food with me so I can wait here as long as it takes. You let me know when you're ready for me to open the tunnel."

"Thank you." Mallory followed Ryan inside, turning to watch the rest join them. "Will we go left or right from the first room?"

They debated their options as they walked to the end of the tunnel. Unable to come to a decision, they tossed a coin and went to the left, Ryan telling them it was north.

Brodie flung open the door. Jumping back, he tripped over Fang, managing to remain upright. "Goblins." He drew two throwing knives.

Mallory launched a fireball at one of the goblins as it entered the room. All three goblins were dead before Ryan could reach them. "If it remains this easy, we will be done before dinner."

"Let's hope we get lucky and it's only a twenty goblin settlement." Ryan searched one of the goblins.

Mallory helped, as did Callum and they managed to find two copper pieces and fifty grams of jerky, which

Brodie added to his belt pouch. They entered the room. It had a pile of broken furniture in one corner, nothing valuable amongst the remains. She looked at the two timber doors that led from the room.

Ryan checked the compass. "North or east?"

"We should go east. North didn't work out too good for us last time." Brodie gestured towards the door.

Callum shrugged. "I don't mind."

Ryan glanced around the group. "We could take turns deciding the direction."

"That sounds like a good idea." Danae glanced at Brodie. "Can I have a turn after Brodie has his?"

Mallory nodded. "Callum can go next then Ryan. I don't mind going last."

"It's okay, I can go last." Ryan turned to Brodie. "East then?"

"East." Once again Brodie opened the door, more cautiously this time, Fang at his heel.

The room led into a corridor and they had the options of turning south along the corridor or opening a door heading north. Danae chose to go south. The corridor led them into another room. There were cobwebs in one corner of the room. Mallory eyed them, wondering if the spiders were as oversized in this world as the crabs and rabbits. If they were, she really didn't want to meet one.

Callum pointed straight ahead. "Might as well keep heading south. Could be safer than opening doors."

They didn't get far before they were faced with going straight ahead, taking a corridor to the west or the door across from it leading east. Mallory looked in each direction then glanced over her shoulder.

"You thinking of going backwards?" Ryan asked.

"No. Checking nothing followed," Mallory said.

"Did you have to say something?" Brodie looked behind. "Now I feel like we're being followed."

"Which way?" Ryan looked at each of the options.

"I think we need to open some doors to actually find anything." Mallory eyed the door heading east. She dreaded what they would find on the other side, but there didn't seem to be anything in the corridors.

Ryan took a step towards the door. "Is that your choice?"

She started to shake her head, nodding instead. "Yeah. We go east again."

Ryan opened the door. "Goblins." He spoke the word softly entering the room and stepping to the side.

Chapter Twenty-Six

Mallory followed Callum, Smudge and Danae into the room, Brodie and Fang on her heels, attacking the moment she was inside. They managed to take out two of the six goblins before they could organise themselves, including a leader goblin. One of the goblins managed to get close to her before she took him out, with Brodie's help. Once the goblins were dead, she stood by one of the two tables looking around the room. "I don't think I want to face more than six at a time."

"I reckon we could easily take on ten." Brodie helped Ryan check bodies.

Mallory joined Callum and Danae who were checking the room. She started with the unlit fire pit since they were looking around the tables. "We don't know what they hit like. That last lot got a little too close. Just because they're short, doesn't mean they don't have a high attack."

"Not even close." Finished searching the goblin, Brodie moved to the next one.

"I think we could manage ten, but more than that and we retreat." Ryan looked at each of them. "Agreed?"

Mallory sighed when both Brodie and Danae nodded, Callum shrugging. It looked like she was outvoted. "Okay, but if it looks like ten are too much, we do retreat."

Between the goblins and the search of the room, they found eight copper pieces, a sheathed dagger, a kitchen knife, two wooden bowls, eight apples and a mortar and pestle. Danae stared at the polished stone objects. "I know I said I didn't want anything…" Her voice trailed off.

Mallory smiled. "I don't mind." With the help Danae had given them, she certainly deserved something.

"Yeah, I don't mind if you have them," Brodie said.

"Majority rules," Ryan said.

Danae picked up the mortar and pestle and put them in her satchel. "Thank you."

Callum glanced around the room. "Which way?"

There were six doors leading from the room. The

one they'd entered and another one further along that wall as well as two to the east, one to the north and one to the south. "That one." Ryan pointed to the north east door.

Brodie, who was closest, opened the door. He peered inside when Mallory moved closer to him. "This corridor only leads to another door. That's no choice. I get to make the next decision."

Ryan moved past him, holding up his lantern. "Okay. We'll check out what's behind that door before you choose the next direction." He went ahead, hooking the lantern handle over his fingers that were wrapped around the hilt of his sword long enough to open the door. "Goblins." He entered the room, stepping towards the side to allow them to follow.

Mallory was relieved to find only four goblins, launching a fireball at one of them, rapidly sending a second one at him. She had no idea who took out the other two, but that left only the fourth one hiding behind a stone tomb. She took a step forward, planning to get closer so she could attack him.

Ryan ran along the side of the room, the light of the lantern he carried splashing over the three chests he passed, and attacked the goblin. Finishing him off, he looked around the room. "Now this is what I expected in a dungeon."

Mallory had to agree. There were three timber chests along each side of the room, the stone tomb in the middle. On the far north east corner was an empty bookcase with a dusty scroll lying on the floor in front of it. She picked up the scroll, unrolling it, frowning as she read over the words.

Danae joined her. "Don't read the words aloud. At least not until everyone else is holding the paper and ready to read them too."

Brodie crowded close. "What is it?"

"It's a crafting ability scroll. It needs to be read aloud and held by the person, or people in a party, who want to unlock that ability." Danae looked up from the scroll, facing Brodie. "I've heard of them, but this is the first one I've seen. I haven't even seen any come into my father's shop and he has a lot of different things for sale."

"That doesn't look like a very useful scroll." Callum came to stand behind them, peering over Mallory's shoulder.

"It doesn't matter if it's useful. This one not only unlocks the ability, but also gives you a CAS point in it. Which will give you one more point towards your next character level," Danae said.

"Can we read it now?" Brodie asked.

Ryan moved in close, taking a hold of the corner of the scroll. "Once everyone is touching the scroll."

Smudge stood in front of them, stretching a paw towards the scroll.

Smiling, Danae patted him on the head. "I'm sorry, Smudge. It doesn't work for animal companions." She moved closer to Mallory, reaching for the scroll.

Mallory felt squished and half tempted to hand the scroll over to someone else to hold. But everyone was touching it and she doubted they'd reshuffle because she wanted them to stop crowding in around her. "Ready?" When everyone said yes, she said, "On the count of three?" Again they agreed and she took a deep breath. "One, two, three. You have unlocked wheelwright, a crafting ability that allows you to repair and make wheels. You have reached level one wheelwright. You now have the ability to make poor quality simple repairs to wheels and can use a hammer." The words vanished from the scroll like they'd never existed as they read them aloud.

Callum took the scroll from Mallory to have a closer look. "That was strange."

"Do you think we'll be able to find more of them?" Brodie glanced around the room, going to the closest chest and opening it.

"It'd be nice if we did." Ryan joined Brodie in checking the chests, Fang trying to peer into the chests too.

"Another four scrolls would be good and then we can go up a character level," Brodie said.

"How are they made?" Callum patted Smudge, who remained close.

Danae shrugged. "I don't know exactly. You need someone of that level crafting ability, a scribe and a mage. I don't know the levels of the other two though. My father was paid to help with a bartering scroll once. I wasn't allowed to go with him to watch."

Mallory checked their stats. Danae was over halfway to her next CAS point and the rest of them only had between twenty-seven and thirty-six experience points. "Maybe having a settlement of fifty goblins won't be too bad if they're scattered around like this. It might give us the chance to gain another CAS point."

"At the most, there'll be another thirty-eight goblins," Ryan said.

"That doesn't sound okay." Callum glanced at Danae. "Although it'd be better if I could one-shot them like Danni frequently does."

Danae smiled, continuing to search the room. The

search gave them another pair of goblin boots and four copper pieces from the goblins. A silver piece was found in a corner of one of the chests.

Brodie looked around the room. "I thought we'd get more from this room because of all the chests."

"I did too." Ryan headed for the door.

They returned to the cooking area and Brodie chose south. It led into an open room with corridors leading off to the west and east, a door to the south.

Danae chose south, glancing at Brodie. "Since we're already going in that direction." She smiled at him.

Brodie returned her smile before stepping forward and opening the door. He stumbled backwards, nearly stepping on Fang who was at his heel. "There's a pit trap in here."

Mallory peered through the doorway, holding her lantern up high. "I wonder what is behind the door south of it."

Callum looked over her shoulder, Smudge once again in his arms. "The only option is south and Brodie already pointed out that if there's no other option you keep going in that direction and it's no one's turn."

Ryan chuckled. "You just don't want to miss out

on your turn." He sheathed his sword. "Let me try going around it."

Mallory watched as he inched his way along the wall and around the trap, having to do the same on the other side of the trap so he could open the door. "What can you see?" She kept her wand ready, prepared to launch a fireball at anything that might come after him.

"Another door leading south." Ryan glanced over his shoulder. "You lot want to join me?" He waited inside the doorway, stepping back as first Mallory reached him, followed by the rest of the group. Smudge and Fang also managed to get around the pit trap, it being too dangerous for them to be carried and both of them refusing to be left behind.

"I really hope we don't have to go back that way," Brodie muttered.

Ryan drew his sword. "I guess it's time to see what's behind the next door."

"I've got it." Callum tried to open the door. "I think it's locked."

"Who's out there?" a voice called from behind the door.

Chapter Twenty-Seven

Mallory shared a look with Ryan, who shrugged. "We're looking for two guards and have a letter for Kruth Blackhelm."

There was a bumping sound followed by a scraping one before the door swung open, an orc peering out. "My brother sent you? I can't think who else would be sending me a letter."

"If you're Kruth." Mallory looked him up and down. He looked very similar to Grotmur. From his height of six and a half feet to his greenish grey skin, bulging arm muscles and protruding lower canines. He wore heavy cotton trousers, a hide vest, leather boots and had a wide copper bracelet on each wrist.

"I'm Kruth."

She tucked her wand into the canvas loop so she could draw the letter out of her satchel. "He was worried about you."

Kruth took the letter. "I was worried about me." He opened the letter, reading it over before meeting Mallory's gaze. "Will you take a letter back to him to let him know I'm alive? I can pay you five copper pieces."

Mallory nodded. It sounded well above what was expected to deliver a letter such a short distance. "We can do that." She took out her wand, feeling vulnerable without it in her hand since they were in a dungeon.

Another orc appeared in the doorway. "That's if we can get out of here."

Kruth turned to the orc. "I told you we shouldn't have tried to open that secret door you found. Nothing good ever comes of looting secret rooms."

"Secret door?" Brodie's expression brightened.

Kruth nodded. "We were caught down the end of a corridor. About thirty goblins between us and freedom. We managed to fight our way through them, may have even taken out one or two, and ran down a corridor that eventually led here."

"Forget standing around talking. We've been stuck in here long enough you're starting to look like a roast dinner." The orc's gaze was fixed on Kruth.

"We'll escort you back to the mine tunnel," Ryan said.

"And you can show us where the secret room is," Brodie said.

"You better not be expecting us to wait around for you to look for the lever." The orc headed out of the room and made his way around the pit trap, Kruth following him.

Within minutes they were back in the room with the corridors leading west and east, taking the corridor heading west. The corridor took a slight turn north then west again and when they reached the end of it, Kruth started to point towards the south. "Goblins. I'll teach them." He reached for his longsword. Before he could draw it, Danae had shot one of the goblins, the second taken out by Callum and Brodie. His sword was half out by the time Mallory threw a fireball at the third one and Danae was taking out the fourth, Callum finishing off the goblin Mallory had attacked.

"That was unexpected." Kruth looked at each of them. "You don't look impressive, but that wasn't bad."

"There's five of them. I'd be more concerned if they didn't do well," the second orc grumbled. "If there was five of us those thirty goblins that attacked wouldn't have stood a chance. Five orcs could have done better than four humans and a half-elf."

Mallory was tempted to argue his comment, but decided it wasn't worth it.

"Where's the secret room?" Brodie asked.

The orc pointed to the south and what looked like a dead end. "We're not looking for the lever. Not unless you brought something for me to eat."

Brodie shook his head, a hand protectively covering his belt pouch. "You'll have to go back to the mine if you're hungry."

While Ryan and Callum checked the bodies, Mallory had a look at the quest update. *Missing Guard: Upon finding Kruth, he asked that you take a letter to his brother. He is willing to pay five copper pieces.* She smiled. They were finally starting to earn some coins and not be constantly spending them. Although they weren't in a town yet. So that was likely to change. Maybe they should stay out of towns and villages for a bit. At least until they'd earned a decent amount of money.

Ryan found two copper pieces, handing them over to Mallory before heading north towards a closed door. They entered a long, narrow room, another closed door at the far end. Callum had barely opened the door when two goblins came at them.

Callum stumbled backwards, dropping his arrow. Mallory took a step towards him, halting when she realised she didn't need to run to his defence. She threw a fireball at one of the goblins. Danae attacked the other one, but he dodged the arrow, Ryan managing to attack him instead. Before Kruth could join the attack, Mallory sent another fireball at the goblin and Ryan finished his off.

Heart still racing, Mallory checked Callum's stats, relieved to find he'd lost no health. "That was close."

Brodie searched a chest that was at the end of a short corridor that headed east while Mallory and Ryan searched the bodies of the goblins. Ryan found a pair of goblin boots.

"What's with all the boots?" Brodie demanded, not having found anything in the chest.

"It's the one thing they really take good care of," Kruth said. "I don't know why they're so particular about their footwear, but they are." He gestured along a corridor that headed directly north from the one they'd been following. "We need to go that way."

The door opened into the room that led to the mine tunnel, the northern door leading from it still open. Mallory looked from one door to the other. "Looks like we took the wrong direction."

"No, we didn't. The direction we took gave us a CAS point," Ryan said.

Mallory smiled. "Okay. We went in the right direction." She turned to Kruth. "There's a dwarf waiting at the boulders. You might want to let him know before you start moving them. No need to have him attacking you. And let him know we need him to wait for us."

Kruth clapped Mallory on the shoulder. "Thanks for coming after us. I'll write that letter to my brother and give it to you when you finish up in here." At her nod, he squeezed through the opening, barely able to fit through. The other orc followed him, giving them a nod and a grunt in farewell.

Brodie didn't wait for them to go before he started speaking. "We should look for the secret door."

"It's not your turn," Callum said.

"But don't you want to find it?" Brodie asked. "It could hide treasure."

"We'll check out the secret room and then Callum can have his turn choosing a direction," Ryan said.

"What happened to voting on it?" Danae asked.

"Don't you want to look for it?" Brodie asked.

Danae grinned. "Well of course."

Ryan chuckled. "Exactly."

They returned to the end of the corridor, going back through the three open doors. Reaching the wall they pressed against it, hit it and examined it. After searching for twenty minutes Danae pushed against a stone that shifted, causing a door to swing open.

When everyone started to head inside, Ryan blocked the way. "What if it's a trap and we get locked in here the moment we're inside? Someone has to wait in the corridor."

"Not me," Brodie said.

Danae looked from the secret room to the corridor. "I should probably wait out here since I can one-shot goblins most times."

Mallory wasn't tempted to disagree, even though she could hear the disappointment in Danae's voice. She really wanted to check out the secret room and from the way her brother kept looking between Danae and the room, he obviously did too.

Brodie grinned. "I'll have a look then come out here so you can have a look."

Danae returned Brodie's grin. "Thank you."

Chapter Twenty-Eight

Mallory cautiously followed Ryan. There were three chests along the western wall and a sconce on the southern wall. An unlit pitch torch rested in it. A search showed that two of the chests were unlocked and empty, the third locked with a rusty iron padlock. Ryan hit it several times with the pommel of his sword before it broke apart and fell on the cracked pavers.

"Lucky we didn't need lockpicks to open it since we don't have any." Brodie pushed open the lid.

Mallory stared at the contents. "Why would anyone store an old robe in a chest?" She could understand storing the potions in the chest, but not the robe.

Brodie peered over her shoulder. "I better go outside so Danni can have a look."

About to gather the contents, Mallory stopped,

waiting for Danae to see them first. Her gaze was drawn to each of the potion vials, not interested in the robe that looked like it wasn't far off being turned into rags. Not that anything else had a chance of holding her attention with the many potions in the chest that were well out of their price range.

Danae looked in the chest, lifting up the cloth. "Mage robe." She held it out to Mallory. "You might find this useful."

Mallory held up the long robe, looking it up and down. "I don't know how useful the robe will be. It'll probably get in the way with how long it is. If it doesn't fall apart first."

"It's armour. Some mages prefer a long tunic and trousers, but many prefer the traditional long robe. It'll be a lot stronger than it looks." Danae knelt in front of the chest, opening up a drawstring cloth bag that had been under the robe.

Mallory folded the robe and put it in her satchel. She'd check it out later, but didn't think she was likely to wear the robe. It'd probably be her rather than Brodie having the dexterity fails if she did. "What did you find?"

"Powdered dragon scale. I'm years away from being able to make potions with this." Danae held out the bag after pulling the strings tight. "You'll make a nice profit from it though. Don't sell it around here. No one could afford it. Unless you offer to exchange it for other items."

"How much is it worth?" Brodie asked from where he stood in the doorway.

"Twenty gold pieces," Danae said.

"That much?" Brodie asked.

"Less than what the robe might be worth," Danae said.

Mallory stared at her. "What?"

Danae smiled. "Is this another one of those times when you didn't understand me or did you not hear me?"

Mallory laughed softly. "I'm not sure. That old robe could be worth more than twenty gold pieces?"

Danae nodded. "A full length mage robe can be worth far more than that. Especially brand new and of a higher quality. Enchanted ones are more costly. From what I've seen come into my father's shop, yours is probably worth about twenty-five gold pieces." She shrugged. "I don't have my father's ability to assess the value of armour so it's only a guess."

Ryan grinned. "Looks like the secret room was worth finding. Now we need to find someone who can afford to buy some of this stuff." He looked at Mallory. "Unless you want to keep the robe."

"I don't think so. I'm not used to long dresses. Or robes. It'd probably get in the way." She gathered up the potions. There were three mana, five health and one cure disease. She gave a health potion to Callum and one to Danae, putting the rest in her satchel, making sure they were separated by the robe so they didn't break. "Now we all have a health potion and some spares." She put the powdered dragon scale in her satchel too.

"Are you finished in there?" Brodie asked from the doorway.

Ryan joined him in the corridor. "Yeah, we should keep moving. It's been over an hour." He grinned. "We don't want to miss dinner."

"Or the extra gold coin," Brodie said.

Mallory laughed, echoed by Ryan and Callum, Danae looking at each of them. She didn't bother explaining that Ryan had been teasing Brodie. She'd learn soon enough how much he enjoyed his food. "Where to now?"

"We should go back to that room with the corridors heading west and east," Callum said. "That's the most logical spot to start from since that's as far as we've been."

Brodie led the way, his pace fast as he headed to the room, Fang on his heels. "Now where? We've been every direction except east. Unless you want to backtrack."

"We go east until there's a decision to be made," Ryan said.

It was only three metres into the eastern corridor that a decision needed to be made. A closed door led north, the corridor finishing in a dead end to the east. The other options were two corridors heading south, both a metre apart. Callum nodded towards the door. "That way. The last door we opened was a good idea."

"It was a secret door. That's different." Brodie swung the door open. "Four goblins." He drew out throwing knives, entering the room.

Mallory followed, the rest on her heels, Fang rushing past her to join Brodie. She tossed fireballs at two of the goblins, the four of them dead within minutes. "It feels almost like cheating." The battle had been over before it had begun. Not long enough for her to worry about any of them being harmed. She supposed she shouldn't become too complacent. There was always the chance they'd stumble upon a horde.

"Ask Kruth. I'm sure he'd tell you goblins are

willing to use overwhelming numbers to take their enemies down." Ryan glanced around the room. "This doesn't look good."

"It looks like it was used by mages of the dark forces." Mallory's gaze was drawn to the two skulls sitting on the altar against the western wall. In front of the altar was a circle carved into the pavers on the floor, symbols carved around the outside of it. The centre of the circle was stained a rusty red.

"Do you think they did human sacrifices in here?" Callum stared at the arcane circle, Smudge leaning against his leg.

Ryan, who was searching one of the two trunks that were against the eastern wall held up a cloth doll, shaking it. "I have no idea, but I found some kid's toy."

Danae took the doll. "Careful. That isn't a toy. It's a poppet."

"A what?" Brodie asked.

Callum frowned. "A medieval doll? A doll is a toy."

"No. A poppet is a cloth doll that's been bound to a particular person to bring harm upon them. If you find one and take it to a Mages Guild or Guardians Guild they'll give you a gold coin in exchange. Every ruler, except those in areas run by the dark forces, has offered a reward of two gold coins for the destruction of poppets. A coin for the finder and a coin for a mage to break the binding without bringing more harm to the person bound to the poppet."

Mallory gently took the poppet from Danae. "How do we transport it so we don't hurt the person bound to it?"

"Create a nest for it in the robe, but don't let the cloth press against the face. The poppet needs to be able to breathe. It'd be better if you had a box with airholes," Danae said.

Mallory did as Danae suggested, keeping the cloth away from the face. She stared at the poppet. "Has blood been used to draw the face?"

"Yes. Either the blood of the person to be harmed or the animal sacrificed in the creation of the binding." Danae searched the other box with Ryan, handing over a silver coin to Mallory.

Brodie winced. "How about we don't talk about how poppets are made and you never ask me to carry one."

Mallory carefully closed her satchel. "How about we find somewhere to hand it in as soon as possible."

"That would be Lilica. The next town east of Simria. There's a Mages Guild there." Danae followed Brodie and Fang from the room, glancing over her shoulder to Mallory. "Your turn to pick a direction."

Chapter Twenty-Nine

After a glance at the satchel, Mallory looked at each of her options. "I guess we go south along the corridor directly opposite this door."

Reaching the end of the corridor, they followed it when it took a sharp turn to the east and again when it turned north. There was a closed timber door in front of them. Brodie reached for the door. "There better not be another one of those dolls in here." He swung open the door. "Five goblins." He stepped inside and to the left, attacking with throwing knives.

Mallory joined Brodie in the room, smiling at the sound of relief in her brother's voice, throwing fireballs at one of the goblins. Before she had the chance to attack any of the others, they were dead. "These must be the easiest quests we've done. Goblins are so easy to take out." A scan of the room showed a lit fire pit in the middle of the room. Across from the door they'd entered was another door. She joined Ryan and Callum who were checking bodies.

"Like training on mudcrabs?" Ryan asked.

Mallory laughed. "I suppose so."

They found four copper pieces, another pair of goblin boots and four large bronze nails. Ryan checked the pocket watch. "An hour and a half. We're doing really good with time." He glanced at Brodie, a grin fleetingly appearing. "Should be back before dinner starts." He tucked the pocket watch in his pocket and picked up the lantern he'd placed on the floor while he'd checked the bodies.

"We don't know how big this dungeon is," Danae said.

"Then we better keep moving." Brodie strode to the next door, waiting for them to join him before he opened it. "More bloody goblins."

Mallory looked across the corridor to the open door of another room. Two goblins came towards them, the third busy patting the rock wall at the northern end of the room. He looked over his shoulder, running after the other goblins, drawing his cudgel as he ran. Mallory threw a fireball at him and Callum shot him with an arrow, causing him to drop mid-stride, the other two goblins already dealt with by their group.

"Reckon there's another secret room?" Brodie pointed to where the goblin had been patting down the wall.

"I'll search the bodies if the rest of you want to see if you can find a lever." Ryan crouched beside the first body, putting the lantern on the floor.

It was Brodie who found it this time, pressing in a smaller rock of the wall, a door swinging open. He started to step inside, moving back to face Danae. "You can go in first this time."

Danae smiled at him. "Thank you."

Mallory followed Danae into the small room. It was two by two metres, three storage barrels along the furthest wall. They found only dust in two of them. Ordinary dust that was of no use to anyone. In the last barrel was six bottles of good wine, according to Danae when she read the label.

"We could sell them?" Mallory asked.

"What's wrong with drinking them?" Brodie demanded from the doorway. Danae swapped places with him and he came in to see the bottles for himself, Fang following. "If we drank them we'd have carrying space for other things."

Mallory laughed. "Nice try. We've got a chest to store them in and we can sell them in Wayholt." She helped Ryan wrap the bottles in the piece of canvas he'd left in the backpack. He'd found no loot on the goblins.

Callum stood guard at the doorway with Danae. "We've killed thirty goblins. At the most, there's another twenty. The place can't be too much bigger."

"There could be areas the goblins are avoiding. Ones taken over by more dangerous creatures," Danae said.

"Great," Brodie muttered.

Mallory agreed with her brother. That was the sort of information she wished Danae could have kept to herself. With the occasional web she'd seen it had her worrying about what type of creatures. After checking on the poppet, which looked fine, she strode for the door. "We better keep moving." She stopped in the corridor, glancing at Ryan. "East or west?"

Before Ryan could reply, two goblins came towards them from the east. Danae, Callum and Brodie finished the goblins off before either Ryan or Mallory managed to attack.

"Thirty-two goblins," Callum said.

Ryan checked the pocket watch. "Two hours. Only two and a half hours left to find the goblin general." He looked in the direction the goblins had come from. "There's a pitch torch burning at the end of the corridor. We might as well see what's down there."

At the end of the corridor was a set of stairs leading upwards on their right and a long narrow room on their left. When Brodie started to go left, Danae tugged on his sleeve and shook her head. She pointed to the stairs. "That's the type of place a general would live in. One set above the rest of his people."

Brodie nodded, leading the way up the stairs.

Mallory followed Brodie, Fang and Ryan. Callum, Smudge and Danae were behind her. Callum carried Smudge and Fang bounded up the stairs at Brodie's side. Only Mallory, Ryan, Brodie and Fang were at the top of the stairs when four goblins came running towards them. The goblins had been in a room at the other end of the corridor, a secret door standing open.

The goblins were dead before they reached them and they checked the bodies for loot. There was yet another pair of goblin boots and five copper pieces. Brodie glared at the boots. "They better be worth something."

Danae laughed softly. "Everything has a value. That doesn't mean you'll be happy with the value of it."

They stepped into the secret room and Mallory scanned the area. There was a door on the western wall, a fire pit on the eastern one in the northern corner with a pitch torch in a light sconce in the corner opposite it. The other corner contained an empty weapons rack and there was a chair directly across from them.

Mallory wrinkled her nose. "What is that smell?"

"The goblins have been in the area too long. We must be close to the general. He would have goblins coming and going at all times, wanting to be near him," Danae said.

"Then let's take him out before he gets some unexpected visitors." Ryan grinned. "Other than us."

Callum opened the door to reveal a three-metre long corridor, a closed door at the end of it. "That's not good. We'll be at a disadvantage."

"One person could open the door and run back here, drawing the goblins towards our room," Brodie said.

"That will put one person in more danger than the rest," Mallory said.

Ryan stepped forward. "I'll do it." He placed the lantern on the floor near her feet, sheathing his sword. "Just make sure you take them out before they reach me." He wrapped his arms around her waist. "At the most, there could be fourteen goblins behind that door. We can manage that many."

"One will be twice as powerful as the rest." Mallory slid her arms around his waist, the backpack pressed against her hands. "Don't go getting killed. It'll be a while before you get another revive."

Ryan chuckled softly before lowering his head, his lips meeting hers. He drew back, looking down at her. "I'll try not to."

"Make sure you don't." She let him go when he drew further away from her, joining the rest of the party near the doorway.

Danae knelt on the floor, half a metre back from the door, her bow aimed down the corridor. Brodie stood behind her, two throwing knives ready. Callum went to Danae's side, kneeling on the floor and readying his bow. Mallory moved to stand behind him, her grip on her wand tightening.

"Everyone ready?" Ryan set the backpack down against the wall. When they nodded, he hurried along the corridor, pausing outside the door before he flung it open and ran back to their room. Unintelligible shouts followed him, the goblins on his heels. There were two normal sized ones and a single goblin that was half a foot taller, brandishing a short sword while the other two carried cudgels.

Chapter Thirty

Mallory flung fireballs at the smaller goblins, wanting to get them out of the way before the larger goblin could reach them, holding her breath as they came closer to Ryan. She guessed Callum had the same idea as he fired arrows at the smaller ones too. When Danae and Brodie attacked the general, she slowly let out her breath. "We should have planned this better." Next time, they would.

Ryan ran into the room and stopped at the side of the door, leaning against it. "What's happening?"

"Only the general-" Mallory broke off as Danae's arrow pierced the general. "All dead." She grinned at him. "We killed the general."

Ryan pushed away from the wall and looked into the corridor. "Callum check the bodies. The rest of us will see what's in the room at the other end." He grabbed the backpack and swung it into place before picking up the lantern he'd left on the floor. "Make sure you get the general's sword."

Mallory was directly behind Ryan when they entered the room so it wasn't until he stepped to the side that she could see it clearly. There was a bed in the corner across from the doorway, a tangle of furs and rags on it. A tattered rug was spread out on the floor, a fireplace in the middle of the northern wall. There was an empty weapons rack in the far north west corner and a chest in the north east one. There was also a pitch torch on both the west and east walls, burning dimly in the wall sconces.

"Not much of a place for their king," Brodie said.

Danae shifted the bedding with the end of her bow. "They rarely have kings. This was only a general." She wrinkled her nose, stepping back from the bed. "I think I found where the worst of the smell is coming from. Uncured hides. If there's anything hidden in the bed I'm not looking for it."

Fang ran forward, sniffing around the bed, tail wagging.

"What's the likelihood of that?" Ryan rose to his feet, a scroll in his hands from the chest he searched.

"Is that another one of those CAS point scrolls?" Brodie asked.

"I haven't had a chance to look yet." Ryan unrolled the scroll, holding it out to Mallory. "It's for you."

She took the scroll and scanned the details. "I wanted to unlock warrior next."

"What's it say?" Brodie tilted her hand so he could read the scroll. "Now that's handy. A level one healing spell."

Callum entered the room, carrying a short sword, Smudge following him. "We have a healing spell now?"

Mallory shook her head. "Not yet. I need to be level one mage to use it."

"Is it any good?" Callum held out three copper and one silver piece.

Mallory took the coins. "It's a heal target spell. One HP for six mana."

"That doesn't sound bad for a low level spell," Callum said.

"I know, but I really wanted to unlock warrior."

"Then unlock warrior next," Ryan said.

"It's logical to gain access to a healing spell as soon as possible." Mallory rolled up the scroll and put it in her satchel, checking on the poppet.

"We have health potions for now. Unlock warrior while you can. There'll always be another spell you want to cast otherwise," Ryan said. "You'll get stuck being only a mage."

"I'll think about it." Mallory turned to Callum. "Is that the general's sword?"

Callum nodded.

"What sort of animal is engraved on the blade?" Brodie came forward to check.

Callum turned the sword towards Brodie. "I don't know if the drawing is a lizard or a snake with legs."

Laughing, Mallory stepped forward to stare at the sword. "No wonder you can't figure it out." The crude drawing had certainly not been made by an artist. She tilted her head to the side, but it made no difference.

"You sure those wavy things near it aren't wings and it's meant to be some kind of drake?" Ryan asked

"Whatever it is, they need a few lessons in how to draw." Callum lowered the sword. "Are we returning the way the orcs returned or are we taking a different path?"

"The quickest way out of here," Mallory said. "I really don't want to get lost." She glanced at her brother. "And be late for dinner." Nor did she want to run into anything worse than a goblin. Such as something that had made those webs.

"Very funny," Brodie muttered.

"I have a couple of beef and vegetable pasties left." Danae frowned when all of them except for Brodie chuckled. "I don't understand."

Mallory struggled not to grin. "Don't worry about it. You'll figure it out."

Ryan checked the pocket watch. "Two hours and forty-five minutes. Let's get out of here before any goblins decide to check on their general."

The corridors they walked through were empty, the only noises were their footsteps echoing around them. Mallory wasn't sure if it was worse taking out goblins in what felt like a cheat, or the silence of the corridors. Before climbing through the hole into the tunnel, she took one last look at the dungeon, only her and Ryan in the room.

"What's wrong?" Ryan, who'd been about to clamber through the hole, stopped and faced her.

"We explored our first real dungeon." A smile slowly formed. "And gained loot."

Ryan chuckled.

Before Ryan could speak, Brodie put his head back through the opening. "Hurry up. It's dark in here and you've got both the lanterns."

With one more glance around, Mallory moved towards the exit. "Out of the way then."

They hurried along the mine tunnel, stopping at

the pile of boulders to call out to the dwarf. "You're finished?" he asked.

"Yeah, we're finished." Mallory couldn't help smiling. Again she thought of the fact they'd completed their first dungeon. It might have been basic, but it was a good start. And they had plenty of loot to sell and some coins. As well as a nice lot of experience points.

The dwarf rolled some boulders out of the way. "You got all of them?"

Callum held up the general's sword. "We killed the general and thirty-eight of his goblins."

Mallory stared at the sword for a moment, mouth open. "Actually, we killed nine of them before we entered the dungeon. The general and forty-seven of his goblins. At the most, there's only one we didn't manage to kill."

"I forgot about adding them in," Callum said.

"I forgot them too," Ryan said. "That other one was probably killed by Kruth and his mate when they were escaping the horde."

The dwarf slowly shook his head. "Killing goblins is so commonplace for you that you struggle to keep track of how many you've killed?"

Ryan chuckled. "Not quite yet, but we're working on it."

While the dwarf led them through the maze of tunnels, Mallory checked their stats, relieved none had lost any health points. Not even Fang or Smudge who were both being carried, curled up asleep in the arms of their companions. The lantern she carried went out. Not that it was a problem with the dwarf's helmet and the lantern Ryan carried. She continued going over the stats. All of them were over halfway to their next CAS point except Ryan, but he wasn't too far off. Danae was the closest to gaining a CAS point, only another twenty-six experience points to earn. Completing the quest would help a bit with that.

As they stepped outside, the darkness not long fallen, Ryan sheathed his sword and checked the pocket watch. "It took us about three and a half hours to do a small, easy dungeon and get back to our starting location."

"An hour to spare," Callum said. "Dinner and an extra gold coin."

Chapter Thirty-One

"Lucky it didn't take longer to find the goblin general." Mallory held up the lantern she carried. "This lantern is out of oil and we left the oil flask in the chest on the wagon."

The overseer hurried towards them, carrying a lantern. "Is that the general's sword?"

Callum handed it over to him. "One goblin general and forty-eight of his goblins if you include the ones that were in the tunnel."

"This is marvellous." The overseer handed the sword to the dwarf, who also took the lantern from Mallory. "See that it's put inside." He gestured towards the stone building. The overseer smiled, his hands spreading wide, the lantern splashing light across the ground in an arc. "My many thanks." He lowered the lantern and fished out six gold coins from his belt pouch. "As promised." He dropped the coins into Mallory's hand.

"What about dinner?" Brodie asked.

"It will be served in less than an hour. You're welcome to go over there now or wait until it's time to dish up," the overseer said. "The wagoner has decided to join me in my dwelling for the evening meal while we finalise our transaction. He drives a hard bargain, but since he brought you lot here to help us out it's a little hard to say no to his demands." The overseer smiled, spreading his hands expansively. "I can't be too upset. Look at all you've done for me." He lowered his hands. "Enjoy the rest of your evening and I'll see you in the morning before you leave."

As they strolled over to the wagon to put Smudge and Fang on the blankets since they both slept, occasionally opening an eye or two to check their surroundings, Mallory brought up her journal to look at the updated quest. *Unwanted Residents Part Two: You not only completed the task, but also met the challenge the overseer set. You were rewarded with six gold pieces for your party. You also earned fifteen experience points each. You have the option of joining the miners for their evening meal.* She smiled. There was no way Brodie would decline the optional reward. Checking the stats she saw Ryan was now over halfway and Danae only needed eleven experience points to gain another CAS point. Maybe she could gather some herbs on the way back to Wayholt. Ryan too.

Callum stretched out on the blanket beside Smudge and Fang, pressed up against the chests on one side. "I don't know about the rest of you, but I could sleep right now. All this walking is wearing me out. And fighting."

"We still have a heap of quests left," Brodie said.

"Only six," Ryan said.

"Exactly." Brodie nodded. "A heap."

Mallory grinned, meeting Ryan's gaze and seeing he grinned too. "That's nothing. Some RPGs I've played I ended up with so many quests I had to delete one before I could take on another."

"Why didn't you complete a quest? Or not bother getting another quest," Brodie said.

"It was a time sensitive quest and I didn't want to miss out on the reward." Mallory sat on the end of the wagon. "Having a wagon would be useful to take with us while adventuring."

"And a fire drake to protect it?" Callum asked.

"How about a travellers caravan? Somewhere dry for when it rains," Ryan suggested.

Mallory glanced skywards. There were plenty of

stars out and the moon was still close to eighty percent visible, only a little smaller than the previous night. "We should get more canvas. Or a tent."

"I need vambraces," Callum said.

"I think we should open one of those bottles of wine," Brodie said.

Ryan chuckled. "I think we shouldn't. Wine is more expensive than ale."

Mallory tuned out the heated debate, checking the poppet was okay. As far as she could tell, it was. Her attention was caught by a change in the tone of the conversation.

"We don't have to do all the quests, but getting a few completed would make the journal look less busy," Brodie said.

"We'd only find more to replace them." Ryan checked the pocket watch. "So there's no rush. But there is for dinner. Fifteen minutes. We should get a seat. Or at least I'm guessing there are seats."

Mallory hopped off the back of the wagon. "Should we leave your companion animals here?" They looked worn out to her.

"Fang hasn't had dinner," Brodie said.

"Neither has Smudge," Callum added.

"We'll bring them leftovers," Ryan said.

"I'll leave the last bone out for Fang in case she gets

hungry." Brodie placed the bone on the ground near the wagon wheel.

"Ready?" Ryan led the way to the long wooden building when everyone nodded.

They ran into Kruth before they could enter, the orc greeting them with a grin and handing over a letter and five copper coins. "You ever looking for a guard, let me know. I'll work at a discounted price. I wouldn't be alive without you lot finding us. We were both getting hungry and I don't know which of us would have won if it had come to a fight to the death."

Mallory took the letter and coins. "Thanks for your offer."

"Any type of guard work would be better than working at a mine. Especially this one in the winter when we're down to a skeleton crew because we're cut off by the snow. My brother is a guard at a store in Wayholt and my sister is a guard for a noble's house in Shadhurst. It'd be great to have a job half as good as theirs," Kruth said. "It's tough being the youngest in the family sometimes."

"We'll keep your offer in mind when we decide on a location to set up a base and if we need a guard," Ryan said.

Mallory checked her journal when an icon

appeared in the corner of her vision. The quest had updated. *Missing Guard: If you are in need of the services of a guard, Kruth is willing to work for you at a discounted rate.*

"Come and I'll find a good table for you. Make sure you have plenty of elbow room." Kruth led the way inside, making some of the miners clear one end of a table. None of them complained and a couple thanked them for dealing with the goblins.

Mallory rose, about to head to where miners and guards lined up to be served their food.

"You sit down. We'll get your food." Kruth gestured to a couple of miners who nodded.

Brodie grinned when they were the only ones left at the table. "I could get used to this."

"I bet you could," Mallory said dryly.

"We've got local rep for here," Callum exclaimed.

Mallory checked her journal. "Five reputation points. That's not bad for a single day."

"You'd think it'd be higher after two quests and killing a lot of goblins," Brodie said.

"It maxes at a hundred. You can't expect it to be too easy to gain." Ryan looked at the miners carrying plates of food towards them. "Here comes dinner."

Brodie's expression brightened. "A roast dinner and

they've filled the plate up. Nice to see they're not stingy with their food."

Mallory eyed the plate put in front of her, thanking the dwarf who delivered it. "I'm not so sure I'm going to get through all of this."

Brodie reached across the table, spearing one of her roast potatoes with his fork. "I'll help." He grinned before popping the food into his mouth.

"I'm sure you will." Mallory slowly shook her head before starting to eat.

By the time the meal was finished, they were full and had leftovers to take back to Smudge and Fang. The wolf cub was chewing on her bone, but happily left it to eat the leftovers while Smudge woke and chirruped excitedly when Callum handed him pieces of roast meat.

The wagoner came towards them before the companion animals had finished eating. "Will you be ready to return to Wayholt in the morning?"

Ryan gave him the pocket watch. "We did everything we needed to in the area."

Chapter Thirty-Two

Mallory's gaze was drawn to the pile of ore covering the fire drake. "Or at least everything we're capable of doing."

"Don't think about it," Brodie warned.

"Think about what?" Mallory asked.

"You're not having a fire drake." He paused a moment. "Although a frost drake might be useful."

"It'll be a long time before we can afford one." Mallory couldn't help looking once more towards where the fire drake was being kept.

"Some adventurers hunt down the nests looking for eggs. As long as you keep them close to the right conditions they'll hatch," Danae said.

"How hard are they to hatch?" Brodie asked. "And how soon after they're hatched can you sell them?"

"How about how long do they take to hatch?" Ryan asked.

"Fire drakes need to be kept warm. You can put them near a fire, but you have to keep turning them and not let them overheat. Frost drakes love the snow and are the easiest to hatch while poison drakes need to be kept damp and warm, but not fire drake warm. Like tropical swamp type of warmth, which is where you find them." Danae looked at each of them. "Are you planning another adventure?"

Ryan grinned. "Always. But I don't think we're quite up to this one yet."

"How hard are they to sell?" Brodie asked.

"I have contacts in Shadhurst," the wagoner said. "If you're interested, I can put you in touch with them for a percentage of the profits from your first lot of hatchlings. They'll give you a fair price, not underpay you like some would."

"What about incubation time?" Callum asked.

"Twenty-eight days," Danae said.

"We'd be stuck in an area till the eggs hatch," Ryan said.

"We'd need a base," Mallory said.

"Or a temporary campsite." Ryan grinned. "Hopefully not too close to the nest."

Danae looked at each of them. "It sounds like you're going to do this."

Mallory wasn't sure how she felt. Was that dread

in the pit of her stomach or something closer to excitement? "I don't know." Again her gaze was drawn to the pile of ore. "I really do want one." And it wasn't like they could afford a drake of any variety any time soon.

"Well trained drakes ride on your shoulder like a parrot," the wagoner said. "They're a lot lighter than they look."

Ryan chuckled. "Keep making comments like that and you'll convince Mallory to go after one."

The wagoner laughed. "Then it benefits me to make such comments since I'd profit from your first sale. A female drake lays anywhere from three to eight eggs at a time. Approximately four times a year. Providing they have a mate and are of breeding age. They can only breed for a short period of time considering they can live for fifty years. They lay eggs from when they're two to ten-years-old."

"Fifty years." Mallory couldn't stop thinking about the fire drake hidden in the cage. "And they can be trained."

"Some people train them to hunt like a falcon, bringing their kill back to share with their owner," Danae said. "We had an adventurer come through Simria one year and he had a frost drake that froze rabbits, bringing them back alive."

"I bet the rabbits didn't appreciate that," Callum said.

Brodie laughed. "How much money can you make on wild hatchlings?"

"Depends on their stats," the wagoner said. "Some are born with good stamina so they can fly further, some are built for speed and others are good at attack. There are a lot of variables. The ones with top stats in nearly every aspect sell for the most."

"I think we've forgotten one major question," Ryan said.

"What is that?" Mallory asked.

"How dangerous are they to go after?"

The wagoner shrugged. "Depends on a lot of things. The area, what else is in the location, how many nests are nearby, the stats of the mother, if she notices you or you get lucky and can raid the nest while she goes on her daily hunt for food." He shrugged again. "I couldn't really say. From mildly dangerous to death defying."

"But we could earn a few hundred gold," Brodie said.

The wagoner looked at each of them, his expression serious. "You decide you want to go after them and I'll put in a word with the hunter. Apparently he saw a fire drake nest on one of his longer treks a few months back. I'll let him know you're to be trusted to pay him a share of the profits. Shouldn't be long and the fire drake will be laying eggs again."

A shiver ran through Mallory and she finally figured out how she felt. Excited. She might be able to have her own fire drake. "I'm interested."

Ryan grinned. "What happened to voting?"

She returned his grin. "Are you saying you're not?"

"I don't think I'd dare." Ryan slipped an arm around her waist, drawing her close. "But it does sound like fun. Exploring a new area, hunting down a nest, sneaking in and taking the eggs and setting up camp somewhere while we protect them and wait for them to hatch."

Callum slowly shook his head. "My brother and his warped sense of fun."

"You don't have to decide right away," the wagoner said.

"I've already decided," Brodie said. "We can make a lot of money. I think we should go after them. Might even get lucky and find a nest with eight eggs."

"I would love to go. Maybe I should apply to postpone going to the academy for a year. Travel around and go on adventures instead. Exploring the goblin dungeon was fun," Danae said.

Mallory tried to think of something to say to Danae to convince her to at least start at the academy. Since her father hadn't wanted her to go on journeys with him she doubted he'd want his daughter to join them on their adventures. "There are other things we need to do first."

"Like what?" Brodie demanded.

"Buy vambraces to start with," Callum said. "And find coffee."

"Who is Coffee?" Danae asked.

"Not who, what." Callum sighed. "I'm beginning to think I'm never going to find anyone who knows if coffee exists on Inadon."

"It's a drink," Ryan said.

"Are we going after a fire drake?" Brodie asked.

"Are we?" Danae looked at them expectantly.

Mallory didn't think she was up to the conversation. There were too many possible problems in encouraging Danae to postpone attending the Alchemy Academy. "We need to make a bit of money to outfit ourselves better first. Especially if we're going to be stuck in an area for a few weeks. And we have to escort the wagoner to Surith."

The wagoner nodded. "Glad you haven't forgotten about that."

"You could take out a loan from a bank," Danae suggested. "They give you a year to pay back what you borrow and charge you twenty percent interest on the balance owing on the last day of each month. If you're late paying your interest they charge you a gold piece a day, but there's nothing to stop you paying your interest early. I'm sure you could find three people willing to write letters of recommendation for you."

"Or join a guild," the wagoner said. "Same terms, but they only charge fifteen percent interest."

Ryan looked at each of them. "It's time for bed. We've got a long journey back to Wayholt tomorrow. Plenty of time to make this decision later."

"I'll sleep on the seat, the rest of you can sort out whether you want to sleep on the wagon or under it." The wagoner drew out his pocket watch, tilting it towards the lantern. "We leaving at eight tomorrow morning? The chests were loaded while you were in the dungeon. The only trading the overseer wanted to discuss with me was selling the fire drake for him. That's too much of a headache for me."

Before anyone could answer, Kruth joined them. "Thought you might want to know one of the older miners said he can feel rain on the way. You might want to make as early a start as possible tomorrow morning if you're to have any chance of beating it."

"Thanks for letting us know," Ryan said.

"Don't forget my offer." Kruth headed off when they nodded.

"I need to write in my notebook before I go to sleep." Mallory rummaged in her satchel, once more checking the poppet was okay. She moved over to the stone building, sitting in the pool of light beneath the lantern hung by the front door.

Chapter Thirty-Three

Mallory stared at the page in front of her, reading over her earlier words before making notes about the current day. It didn't take long to write a paragraph and Ryan joined her while she cleaned the pen nib with the calico cloth and packed away her notebook, being careful of the poppet. "What's wrong?"

"Nothing." He sat beside her, his back against the wall, the whetstone in one hand, his sword in the other. "We need to head to the mainland and start making connections over there. Like we're doing here. As soon as we have enough money to begin sorting out our own place."

"Do you think we should take out a loan?" Undoing her plait, she used the hairbrush.

Ryan ran the whetstone along the blade of his sword. "Not unless we get desperate."

"What about Danni joining us instead of going to the academy?" She worked on a knot, wincing.

Ryan grinned. "A bow wielded by an irate father would probably hurt as much as a shotgun wielded by an equally annoyed father."

She laughed softly, about to return the hairbrush to her satchel. "Pretty much my thought. Except it didn't involve weapons, only reputation."

Ryan sheathed his sword and took the hairbrush from her. He removed the hair band before he ran the brush through his hair. "I don't think Brodie will agree."

"We don't need any more problems." She thought of Fang. "I'm not sorry we rescued Fang, but do you think hellions will figure out we were the ones who killed some of their members?" She plaited her hair as she spoke.

Ryan shrugged. "I don't know. I guess we'll find out sooner or later."

"Hopefully later. After we have the chance to level up." Finished plaiting her hair, she rose to her feet, taking the hairbrush Ryan held out. "We should probably get some sleep if we plan to leave at first light."

The lantern was off when they returned to the wagon and Danae was stretched out between the chests. She lifted her head, a shadowy movement in the night. "We're up here, Mallory. The wagoner put a canvas over the top at the other end. We can draw it further over the chests if it gets too cold. Or it rains."

Mallory clambered up onto the wagon, stretching out beside Danae. "Let's hope we get lucky and it doesn't rain until we're back in Wayholt." She frowned. "Why don't we have any blankets?"

"Because you got the wagon bed," Brodie said from beneath the wagon. "It's cold down here."

"Can Smudge sleep up there with you?" Callum asked. "I don't want him to get cold."

"And Fang too," Brodie said.

It took them a few minutes to get organised, Fang and Smudge snuggling in between Mallory and Danae. Mallory fell asleep patting Fang, who was closest to her, woken at daylight by a cold nose pressed against her cheek. She pushed the wolf cub away from her face. "Do you have to?"

Fang went to the edge of the wagon looking between Mallory and the ground.

Danae half sat up. The canvas was pulled over the chests so there wasn't much head space. "It's morning already?"

Mallory didn't bother answering, clambering out of the wagon and helping Fang down. It didn't feel like morning. She could have done with a bit more sleep. She yawned, wrapping her arms around herself. "I'd hate to think what it's like around here in winter."

Danae joined her, arms also wrapped around herself. "I should have brought a jacket."

Ryan crawled out from beneath the wagon. "How about we have a few apples for breakfast and get on the road. It's warmer at Wayholt."

Callum staggered out. "I'd kill for a coffee. And not just goblins."

"I have some pasties left." Danae turned back to the wagon to get her satchel.

Brodie came out from under the wagon. "How many?"

Mallory caught Ryan's gaze, laughing softly when she saw his grin.

"One each." Danae took one out from her satchel and handed it to Brodie.

It didn't take them long to get ready for the morning. Brodie also had two apples along with his beef and vegetable pastie and the overseer came out to once more ask the wagoner if he was interested in selling the fire drake for him. Kruth also came to see them off.

Danae rode beside the wagon on Augusta and the

canvas had been rolled halfway back, ready to be pulled over the chests if it should rain. Which it did over an hour into their journey. It had given all of them, except for Mallory, enough time to gather herbs so Danae could gain a CAS point and the rest of them managed to catch up to Mallory's experience points of seventy-eight. Danae's saddlebags and satchel were full of herbs along with the chest and basket.

Mallory was squished between Danae and Callum, the three of them lying in the back of the wagon, the soft sound of rain on the canvas above them, Augusta tied to the back of the wagon. Ryan and Brodie sat beside the wagoner on the seat, their gear in the wagon behind the seat along with Fang. Smudge was on the seat, enjoying the rain, making chirruping noises.

Callum stared out the back of the wagon. "We really need to go home. Even if it's only so I can grab a cup of coffee."

Mallory grinned. "It hasn't been that long."

"Long enough for me to have a headache," Callum said.

Mallory's grin vanished. "Are you serious?"

"I wish I wasn't. My head is killing me. Worse than last time."

"I keep telling you it's past time you cut back," Ryan called out from the front of the wagon.

Danae frowned. "I thought you said you have to figure out somewhere to live."

Mallory hesitated. "We're not exactly from this world."

"Oh, you use demonic magic to travel between worlds. I haven't met many people who've done that. It's pretty expensive," Danae said. "I'd love to travel between worlds."

"Maybe-" Brodie was abruptly cut off. "Ow. Quit it, Ryan."

Mallory tried not to smile. She had no idea how they could explain Danae, with her slightly pointed ears, if they took her home with them. She met Callum's gaze. "Can you last long enough to get back to Buckneth?"

Callum groaned, resting his head on his hands. "We're not likely to get back until tomorrow."

"Have some wine, that'll cure your headache," Brodie called out.

"And give me a bigger one later," Callum said. "I've really got to figure out how to bring coffee here."

Mallory rested a hand on his shoulder. "How about having a bit more sleep?"

The wagon slowed and Callum looked towards the front of it. "What's going on out there?"

Mallory eyed the rain that was steadily falling, not sure if she wanted to get wet so she could see what was happening.

"Stay in the wagon for now," Ryan said. "There's a man coming towards us on horseback. I'll let you know if he turns out to be a threat."

Mallory drew out her wand, twisting and turning to be able to do so in the cramped space between the chests. "I hate not being able to see what's going on."

"So do I," Callum said. "At least your weapon's easy to get. Danni and I will need a few minutes to get ours since they're between the canvas and the chests."

"Keep it down, he's getting close," Ryan said.

Mallory stared out the back of the wagon, remaining silent, hearing only the patter of rain on the canvas. She leaned her head close to Callum's so she could whisper in his ear. "I wonder what the travellers' caravans are like."

He turned so he could also whisper. "I'm guessing like a mediaeval one. Made of timber with a rounded roof. And probably a lot more comfortable than this."

Chapter Thirty-Four

Mallory opened her mouth to reply, her words remaining unspoken when she saw the man ride past. With his armour and sword at his side, he had to be a warrior. Behind him was another horse carrying two panniers. She waited until he was a fair distance from them before she spoke. "That's what we need. A packhorse with those baskets. Look how much extra space we've needed this time." She glanced at the chest beside her that was filled with their gear.

Callum turned to Danae. "Do you think we could swap any of the more expensive things at the stables?"

"Maybe. The stable owner has a lot of dealings with the apothecary if any of the horses get sick. He might be interested in the powdered dragon scale."

"We could get a horse?" Brodie asked.

"Not a horse, but possibly a donkey," Danae said.

"The powdered dragon scale wouldn't be enough to buy a horse."

"I'd be happy with a mule," Callum said.

Danae laughed softly. "No, you wouldn't. Believe me when I say 'stubborn as a mule' came about for a reason."

"We should get in before midday," the wagoner said. "That'll give you plenty of time to see what you might be able to buy. I can sell off the rest of your goods if you want. Not the mage robe though. You'll either have to sell it in a larger town or take goods in exchange. Nor will I charge you a percentage of the sale. What you did at South Peak Mine gained me a better deal with the overseer."

"If we get in that early, we could head back to Buckneth this afternoon," Callum said.

"Well now," the wagoner said. "Wouldn't want to leave it too late. You never know what we might encounter along the way."

Silence fell at his words and Mallory wondered what the rest of them were thinking about. The hellions, like she was? She had no idea and didn't want to ask in case they were. She really didn't want to remember, let alone talk about, dying at the hands of the hellions. Wriggling, she returned her wand to the loop of canvas, trying to get comfortable again once she'd finished putting it away.

The repetitive sound of rain on the canvas and the rumble of the wagon sent Mallory to sleep and she didn't wake until the wagon was no longer moving. She tried to stretch, having no luck in the cramped space. "Where are we?" She blinked as she attempted to focus on the view out the back of the wagon. It took her a few seconds to realise the rain had stopped even though the day remained overcast.

"Wayholt." Ryan drew back the canvas to halfway along the wagon, Brodie on the other side helping.

Mallory sat up. "You're drenched." She looked from Ryan to Brodie. "Both of you."

"You should have seen us before." Ryan grinned. "We've dried out a bit since the rain stopped."

Danae hopped out of the wagon. "Are we leaving this afternoon or in the morning?"

The wagoner joined them at the back of the wagon, taking out his pocket watch. "It's not quite midday. I reckon I can have everything sold within the hour, eat the midday meal, catch up with a couple of people and be ready to leave by one-thirty. As long as we're away from here by two at the latest, that should give us enough time to reach home before dark. I'll meet you at the tavern once we're all done."

Mallory winced as she got out of the wagon, her legs cramped after being squished in for so long. "Will that give us enough time?"

Danae nodded. "If we're quick. Most of my stuff is packed and ready to go since the first time I was meant to leave. Have you got the powdered dragon scale?"

Mallory grabbed her satchel out of the wagon. "Yeah."

Ryan rummaged around in the chest, taking some of the items out and returning them to the backpack. "The gear left in the chest can be sold."

"Better not have taken out any of the goblin boots," Brodie muttered.

Ryan grinned. "You sure you don't want a pair for a souvenir?"

"As if."

Mallory laughed at her brother's expression. She glanced around the area realising they were across the road from the stables. "We better get on with it if we plan to be out of here before two." She wasn't sure they could manage since there were a few things they needed to do.

Danae gathered the reins of her horse and walked beside Mallory. "Did you want me to see what I can do about getting you the trade you want? The stable owner knows me and will probably give me a better deal than he'd give strangers."

Mallory nodded, handing over the powdered dragon scale. "A donkey and two panniers would be great."

"I'll see what I can manage." Danae gave the reins to Brodie to hold.

They waited out the front of the stables for Danae. Mallory paced back and forth, stretching her legs after being stuck in the wagon for so long. "I don't know what's worse. Being in the wagon or walking."

"I guess it would depend on the wagon. That one's not very comfortable with how crowded it is," Callum said.

"I've been thinking about a travellers' caravan ever since Danni mentioned them." Mallory grinned. "I'm betting they're going to be way out of our budget."

Ryan chuckled. "More than likely, but they might be worth looking into later."

"Would there be real beds in one?" Brodie asked.

Mallory stared at him for a moment. "No complaints about how much they'd cost?"

"After sleeping on the ground at the mine, I'd almost be willing to go into debt for a caravan if it meant a comfortable bed," Brodie said.

"I'm with you on that one," Callum said.

Mallory looked from one to the other. "You both want a caravan." She could hardly believe what she was hearing. Her brother was happy to spend money on something other than food.

"You know, it might not be so bad," Ryan said. "It'd probably save us on the cost of staying at taverns and inns when the weather gets colder."

"I don't want to think about winter and being on the road with limited gear," Mallory said.

"You could also get one of those enchanted box things that Danni mentioned if we had a caravan," Brodie said. "To store our food in so it lasts longer."

Mallory laughed. "I should have known."

"We all should have known." Ryan chuckled. "Everything is always related to food."

Brodie glared at them. "It is not."

Danae came out when they were all laughing, frowning as she looked at each of them, her gaze resting on Brodie last. He was still frowning. "What's wrong?"

Brodie shook his head, gesturing towards the stables. "Is he interested in the trade?"

Danae shrugged, taking the reins back from Brodie. "He sent his stableboy to discuss things with the apothecary. It'll give us time to go to my place and get everything sorted out there. My mother will probably give us something to eat."

"What are we waiting for?" Brodie asked.

"We should deliver the letter first," Mallory said. "Grotmur is worried about his brother. We should let him know he's okay."

"We don't know where he works," Callum said.

"I know. He works at the trading post. Grotmur stays out the back so he doesn't frighten the customers," Danae said. "Did you want to go there first?"

They all nodded and followed Danae as she led them to the trading post and around the back of the building. Grotmur smiled when he saw them. "You spoke to him? You gave my brother the letter?" He nodded as he spoke. "Yes?" His tone was hopeful.

Chapter Thirty-Five

Mallory drew out the letter from Kruth, handing it over, relieved she didn't have bad news for Grotmur. "Your brother's safe now."

Grotmur took the letter, opening it up, his lips moving as he read it. He looked at them. "You saved my brother's life. How can I ever thank you? I don't know how many times I've told him that job wasn't for him. Being a guard at a mine is one of the worst possible jobs. Extremely dangerous."

"He survived being attacked by thirty goblins," Brodie said. "I reckon he did pretty good."

Grotmur slipped the letter into a pocket. "Thirty. That's terrible." He held out five silver pieces. "I feel like I should be paying you far more than this, but it's all I can afford."

Mallory took the coins. "It's more than enough.

We were happy to help. And Kruth is a lot more capable than you think he is."

"You don't know him like I do." Grotmur slowly shook his head. "He tends to end up in impossible situations. This is only the latest."

Mallory opened her mouth to stick up for Kruth. Before she could say anything, Ryan spoke.

"We better get moving. We're heading back to Buckneth this afternoon."

"Don't let me keep you. You don't want to be on those roads after dark," Grotmur said. "And thank you. My family and I are grateful for all you've done."

Danae led the way. "We'll go to my mother's now. That should give the stable owner enough time to decide if he's interested in the trade."

While she followed Danae, Mallory checked the details of the quest they'd finished. *Missing Guard: Grotmur was grateful you not only delivered his letter, but escorted his brother to safety. As well as the five copper pieces you received from Kruth, you were rewarded with five silver pieces for your party. You also earned twenty experience points each. You have the option to hire Kruth as a guard at a discounted rate.* Mallory laughed. "We were tricked into doing an escort mission."

"There seems to be a lot of them to be done around here," Callum said.

Mallory checked her stats. "Ninety-eight XP. We'll gain another CAS point when we reach Buckneth this afternoon and complete another quest."

"We could gather herbs along the way," Brodie said.

"That will depend on if we can get a donkey to carry our gear," Ryan said. "We don't have space for too many herbs. Not with all the gear we've been getting along the way."

Danae stopped at a timber cottage, tying her horse to a post out the front before she opened the door. "I'm home."

Mallory followed Danae inside, her companions behind her, surprised to find the cottage to be in better shape than any others she'd been in so far. The room was large enough to have two chairs by a fireplace at one end, a kitchen table and four chairs across the room from them. There was a cooking fire in the middle and the floor was paved with stone. Next to the cooking fire was a brick oven, a chimney rising through the roof. Along the wall to the right was a timber cupboard and a bench, a door beside them. The door opened, showing a room with two timber beds, a chest between them. A tall, pale skinned woman with fine features, pointed ears and blond hair stood in the doorway. Her eyes were the same colour as Danae's. An impossibly pale green.

She looked at all of them crowding around her daughter. "Did you manage to gather the herbs you were interested in?" Her gaze came to a rest on the bow and quiver of arrows Danae carried. "Or did you have a different plan, one you did not bother to inform me of?"

Danae laughed softly. "Both." She went forward to hug her mother. "I'm unharmed and safe." She drew out the mortar and pestle from her satchel. "And I have something that will help me at the academy."

"You will still attend?" Her mother looked at each of them again. "You don't plan to remain with your party?"

Danae returned the mortar and pestle to her satchel. "I'm planning to attend the Alchemy Academy. I want to learn everything I can about herbs and potions." She glanced at her party. "But I also want to have some more adventures in between learning." Danae drew her mother towards the door. "Come and meet my friends." Danae introduced each of them, gesturing to her mother last. "This is my mother, Sarisa."

Sarisa inclined her head before turning back to her daughter. "When do you leave?"

"As soon as I'm packed and we've eaten." Danae glanced at Mallory. "They'll escort me to Surith, by way of Buckneth, where I can catch a ship to Simria."

Sarisa didn't answer immediately. "I would rather you waited for those who were originally going to escort you to your father."

"I'm not about to go anywhere with them. What if they changed their mind again because something better came along? I might not get to Merrow in time," Danae said.

Once again Sarisa was silent for a moment. "You gather your gear and I'll set out the midday meal." She turned to Mallory and her party. "If you want to bring the two chairs from beside the fire to the table." Without waiting for a reply, she strode to the cupboard set along the right hand side of the room.

Brodie was the first to move, collecting one of the chairs and sitting at the table. Ryan brought the other one over while Sarisa busied herself filling plates with food at the bench. Once she was finished, she beckoned Callum over to help her serve. Both companion animals watched the plates being brought to the table, Smudge making excited sounds when Sarisa put a bowl of diced fish in front of him. Fang yipped when she was given a bowl of diced meat.

"Thank you." Mallory met Sarisa's gaze. "The food looks great."

"You will take care of my daughter and see she arrives safely. She's far too adventurous for my peace of mind," Sarisa said.

Mallory nodded. "We'll take her to Surith and protect her along the way."

"What do you want in exchange?" Sarisa asked.

"Exchange for what?" Mallory frowned.

"I think she's talking about payment for taking Danni to Surith," Ryan said.

"Oh." Mallory shook her head. "We don't need anything. She's our friend."

"Food," Brodie said. "For the journey."

Sarisa inclined her head. "I can also offer you a couple of recipes if you're interested."

"Cool," Brodie said. "I've only got one level in cooking though. But I'm thinking of putting another level or two into it."

"I'll keep that in mind when choosing recipes." Sarisa strode into the other room, disappearing out of sight when she turned to the left.

Mallory was tempted to lean back in her chair to see if Sarisa was visible. She managed to control the urge and continued eating the food set in front of her. It was far better than their attempts at cooking.

Danae headed outside with a bundle wrapped in a blanket and tied with rope, two blankets rolled up together under her other arm. She returned minutes later without either the bundle or blankets and joined them at the table. "We can go as soon as we've eaten."

"Your mum said she'd pack us some food for the journey," Brodie said.

"Oh, I forgot about that. It's a good thing you remembered." Danae smiled at Brodie.

Mallory tried not to laugh. She ended up making a strangled sound that worsened when she caught sight of Ryan's grin. She cleared her throat. "She wanted to make sure we'd take you safely to Surith."

Danae laughed softly. "I'm sure she did."

"We'll make sure you arrive there safely," Ryan said.

"Don't worry, we'll come to Eridell soon," Brodie said.

Danae grinned. "I'll look forward to your arrival."

Sarisa came out of the room, several folded pieces of paper in her hand. She placed them on the table. "Flatbread is a level one recipe, as is grilled fish. Venison stew is level two and bread is level three." She placed two silver pieces on top of the recipes. "To help with the cost of food along the way. I'll pack some beef and vegetable pasties to see you through the evening and for breakfast tomorrow. I'm afraid I don't have more than that to spare."

Chapter Thirty-Six

Mallory slipped the coins in a pocket and the recipes in her satchel. "This is more than enough. Thank you." As soon as they'd finished eating, she stacked the empty plates.

Sarisa handed a calico sack to Ryan, turning to Mallory. "Leave the plates there. I'll deal with them later. You'd best be on the way so you've plenty of time to reach Buckneth before dark." Sarisa walked with them to the front door, hugging her daughter and kissing both of her cheeks. "Write to me, when you reach Surith, and have your father let me know you have arrived in Simria." She dropped some coins in Danae's hand. "I want to know you're safe."

Danae put the coins in her belt pouch. "I will." She smiled. "I'll miss you. Are you sure you won't visit me in Eridell?"

Sarisa shook her head. "This is my home. Where

my roots are. Maybe one day you'll return and see you belong here too."

Danae kissed her mother on each cheek. "I think I have my father's wanderlust."

"He found his place eventually," Sarisa said. "You will too one day."

Danae smiled, heading to her horse without a reply. She untied her horse and with a wave for her mother, strode towards the stables.

Mallory also waved to Sarisa, wishing there was something she could say to the elf to make her look less sad. But unless she could convince Danae to stay with her mother, she doubted anything else would cheer Sarisa.

When they reached the stables, they once again stayed out the front, Brodie holding the reins of Augusta. He stared after Danae. "Do you think the stable owner will agree?"

Mallory shrugged, smiling when she noticed Ryan did the same. "I have no idea." She looked her brother up and down. "Should you change out of those damp clothes?" She turned to Ryan. "You too?"

This time it was Brodie who shrugged. "They'll dry. Eventually. They aren't as bad now. At least we're not dripping all over the place. Like we were earlier."

"It's not like we've got anywhere to dry them. Like a clothesline or something," Ryan said.

Danae came outside, grinning. "He has a jenny available. He's willing to trade the donkey, two panniers, a halter, a lead rope and two gold pieces for the powdered dragon scale. What do you say?"

"Is that good?" Brodie asked.

"About as good as you're going to get around here," Danae said. "I don't think you could do much better in a larger town. You might have done better in the capital if you found an honest trader."

"We'll take it," Ryan said.

"Is that a yes or do I have to wait for the majority thing?" Danae asked.

"Yes from me," Callum said.

Mallory nodded at the same time as her brother agreed.

"I guess that's the majority rules then," Danae said.

Ryan chuckled. "We call it unanimous."

Danae nodded. "Unanimous." She headed back inside the stables returning a few minutes later leading a donkey with two panniers, one on either side of her body.

Mallory took the lead rope Danae held out to her. "What's her name?"

"She hasn't got one. You'll have to name her." Danae took the reins from Brodie.

"Do we need to add her as a companion animal?" Mallory asked.

Danae led the way towards the tavern. "You can, but it isn't necessary. You can have pets and livestock without them needing to be companion animals."

"I don't know what to call her." Mallory ran a hand down the donkey's neck. "She's very pretty."

They stopped at the front of the tavern and Ryan took off his backpack. "I'll put some of this gear into the panniers if someone wants to go in and let the wagoner know we're here."

"I can," Callum said.

At the same time, Brodie also said, "I'll do it."

Danae handed the reins to Mallory. "I'll go with them. I wouldn't mind saying goodbye to a few people."

Mallory looked from the reins to the lead rope that she held, her gaze drawn to the three figures disappearing inside the tavern. "Should we be concerned?"

Ryan chuckled. "Brodie in a place with both food and alcohol. More than likely."

"That's what I thought."

Ryan slipped the backpack into place. "I'll take the

reins and lead rope if you want to run in and get the money off the wagoner before Brodie tries to spend it." He held out his hands.

"Thanks." She handed over the reins and lead rope before hurrying inside. She reached the table in time to see the wagoner draw out some coins and place them on the table. Picking up her pace, she was able to scoop up the coins before Brodie could, needing both hands to gather them. "Thank you. Did you manage to sell everything?"

"Two daggers, six bottles of wine, five pairs of boots, bone dust, all the herbs and the nails. Thirty-six gold pieces, one silver piece and six copper pieces. The majority of it was for the wine and boots."

"For the boots," Brodie said.

Mallory smiled at the disbelief in his tone. "Aren't you glad you didn't drink the wine and we got so many boots?" She'd barely managed to glance at the coins, had been too worried about Brodie spending them. Although at this rate, that might not be a problem.

"Do we get any of that to spend?" Brodie asked.

"We'll vote on it," Mallory said. When her brother opened his mouth to speak, she quickly added, "When we're all together."

The wagoner stood up. "We ready to go?"

"Yeah," Callum said. "We got everything done. Including buying a donkey."

They traipsed outside, the wagoner asking them about the animal. Danae was able to tell him the donkey was five-years-old. The rest of them couldn't tell him much other than it was a jenny and grey coloured with white around the muzzle as well as along the inside of the legs and up to the belly and across to the chest.

The wagoner checked over the donkey, nodding his head as he ran his hands over her. "Fine animal. Eleven hands high. Good health. You did well."

"Danni did well," Mallory said.

"The stable owner here is honest. It's easy to trade with an honest person," Danae said.

The wagoner nodded. "It certainly is." He glanced over his shoulder. "My wagon is out the back. I'll collect it and meet you here in a couple of minutes." When they agreed, he strode around the side of the building.

While they waited for him, Brodie asked Danae about Elvish and she taught them how to say hello, laughing at their attempts. As each of them finally managed to pronounce the word properly, it unlocked languages for them. Mallory checked her journal once she'd finally said the word correctly, smiling at Callum's attempts. *You have unlocked languages, a crafting ability that allows you to speak, write and communicate in the various languages of the sentient races.*

"It's odd how they're all called crafting abilities," Ryan said.

"Crafting is creating something with skills. Can you not create better sentences and communicate more easily by improving your abilities in languages?" Danae asked.

Before Ryan could comment, the wagoner came around the corner in his wagon, slowing as he came alongside them. Ryan jumped in the wagon, holding the lead rope of the donkey that obediently followed behind. "No need to stop. We've all got in and out of the wagon while it's been moving." He tied the lead rope to the back of the wagon.

Mallory, Callum and Brodie clambered in while Danae rode alongside them. They were barely seated before Brodie asked about voting on sharing some of the coins.

"How much do we have now?" Ryan asked.

"Forty-eight gold, thirty-two silver and sixty copper pieces," Mallory said.

"That's a lot. Can we each have some now?" Brodie asked.

"There are heaps of things we need," Ryan said.

"Like what?" Brodie demanded. "We've got a donkey."

"I need vambraces," Callum said.

"Vambraces would be nice," Danae said.

"After we get vambraces can we start splitting the money?" Brodie asked.

Chapter Thirty-Seven

Mallory tried not to laugh at her brother's expression. It had gone from argumentative to accepting in a few seconds.

"We need bags and cloth sacks to store things in before we put them in the panniers. To make it easier to find them and get out what we need," Ryan said. "Everything is looking jumbled in them at the moment."

"The weaver who lives next door to me makes both rough and fine sacks and bags," the wagoner said.

"We could collect some of the herbs she uses for dye," Ryan said. "She might exchange some bags for the herbs."

"The herb is calendula," Callum said.

Brodie's expression brightened. "Some XP and saving coins. Does that mean we can buy dinner at the tavern tonight?"

Mallory glanced at each of them, slowly nodding. "We should buy dinner tonight. To celebrate our first successful dungeon."

Brodie nudged Callum. "You better vote yes."

Ryan chuckled. "I say yes too."

Callum shrugged. "I'd rather a litre of coffee, but dinner sounds okay."

Mallory looked Callum over. "Still have a headache?"

"Yeah." He gestured to herbs growing not far from the road. "Who is picking the first lot of calendula?"

"I am." Brodie jumped out of the wagon, hurrying over to the plant.

Ryan jumped out of the wagon too. "Grab vegetables. We don't have any left."

"But we're eating at the tavern tonight." Brodie dropped the herbs into one of the panniers on the donkey.

"There are other meals to think about." Ryan ran back to the wagon with two carrots, adding them to the pannier.

The next hour they spent gathering calendula, carrots, potatoes and onions. As well as plenty of herbs, they also found four carrots, ten potatoes and three onions. Mallory, Ryan, Brodie and Callum also gained a CAS point.

Danae hadn't helped gather anything, only laughed softly when Brodie asked her to give them a chance to catch up. Brodie sat on the seat beside the wagoner, looking through the recipes he'd asked Mallory to give him, Fang curled up on his lap. "I'm going to level up my cooking. I want to use these recipes." He paused a moment, frowning. "I didn't learn anything new. It just told me I levelled up."

"At least you can use those recipes now," Callum said. "I still have no idea what to put my points into."

"Even if I put both my points into hunting, I'm one point short to be able to use a hunting bow," Ryan said.

Mallory didn't know if she should add hers into alchemy yet or wait and see what else she needed to level up. "Are you putting the points in now, Ryan?"

He nodded. "You have reached level three hunting. You are five percent more likely to spot tracks." He paused a moment. "You have reached level four hunting. You now have the ability to use a campfire to make poor quality food."

"Spotting animal tracks and cooking on a campfire are useful," Brodie said. "Especially if we end up camping out trying to get fire drake eggs." He patted Fang when she whimpered. "What's wrong, girl?"

Mallory scanned the area, a curve in the road ahead

of them. She frowned. "I think we're close to where she lost her family."

Smudge, who'd been sleeping curled up on the back of the wagon, sat up and made his high-pitched warning sounds.

They grabbed weapons, jumping off the wagon, and in Danae's case, dismounting. The wagon came to a stop and the wagoner drew out his brass spyglass. "I can't see anything."

Ryan held out his hand. "Can I borrow it? I can go ahead and have a look."

The wagoner started to hand over the spyglass, putting it to his eye when three men came around the corner. "A hunter and two warrior hellions. The hunter is hobbled. I'd say he's their prisoner."

Callum put an arrow to his bow, striding forward so he was in front of the wagon, Danae at his side doing the same. "How much health?"

"The hellions are level three warriors. Thirty-five health points each. The hunter has no level. Obviously hasn't chosen a class. He has nine health. Could be injured." The wagoner lowered the brass spyglass when the hellions began to run towards them.

Flashes of the last fight against hellions ran through Mallory's mind and she tried to push them aside, her grip tightening on her wand. No wonder she hadn't survived against them with that amount of health. Taking a deep breath, she launched a fireball at the hellion on the left.

Ryan remained beside Mallory. "Everyone focus on the left one. If we can take one out before they reach us it'll make the fight easier."

Danae, who'd shot the one on the right, aimed at the one on the left. She fired at the same time as Callum, Mallory sending another fireball at the hellion, while Brodie threw two knives at him.

The wagoner looked through the brass spyglass again. "He's at eight health. The one on the right has thirty."

"Danni and Mallory finish off the one on the left, Callum and Brodie focus on the second one." Ryan ran towards the hellions who were only metres away. Fang jumped off the wagon seat, running towards the hellions too.

Mallory followed Danae's arrow up with a fireball, relieved it was enough to take out the hellion. She focused on the second one, who was attacking Ryan with two short swords.

"Kill him before he can hurt Fang." Brodie kept throwing knives at the last hellion.

Mallory breathed in sharply when the hellion got past Ryan's sword, blood darkening his shirt.

Callum drew back an arrow, aiming at the hellion. "You picked the wrong day to attack. I've been too long without coffee."

Callum's words startled the hellion who blocked Ryan's attack as he glanced at Callum. "You're from Cape Barren?"

"What-" Callum broke off as a fireball struck the hellion at the same time as an arrow from Danae found its mark. The hellion dropped to the ground. Callum lowered his bow, easing the string back into place so he could remove his arrow from it. "What did he mean?"

Mallory ran towards Ryan, opening the journal to check his health. He was down to eleven. She slipped her wand into the canvas loop, grabbing hold of him. "You okay?"

Ryan breathed heavily. "I could do with a little less pain."

Danae joined them, holding out the waterskin of health tea that had been in the wagon. "Drink a cupful. It'll help with the pain because it'll start the healing."

Brodie knelt in the dirt, checking Fang over and telling her how good she was.

Still holding onto Ryan, Mallory glanced around the area. There were no more hellions, but there was the hunter. He'd fallen in his attempt to escape and was struggling to rise again.

Ryan sheathed his sword, smiling at Mallory before he drew away from her slipping his hand in hers. He squeezed lightly. "I'll be okay." Letting go of her hand he took the waterskin from Danae. "Does someone want to help the hunter?" He raised the waterskin to his mouth. "Other than Danni."

Mallory nodded. "I'll go." She took a step away from him. "You sure you'll be okay?"

Ryan lowered the waterskin, nodding. "Go on. Danni will remain beside me and shoot the hunter if he goes to attack you. She tends to get more crits than the rest of us."

Mallory slowly walked towards the hunter, who was now on his feet and warily watching her. "I can cut the rope they used to hobble you." She gestured towards her dagger, leaving it sheathed. "My name is Mallory, what is yours?"

"You're the ones they're looking for, aren't you?" The hunter took a step backwards.

Chapter Thirty-Eight

Mallory stopped. "We have no plans to hurt you. And what do you mean we're the ones they're looking for."

"The hellions have been looking for the people who killed three of their friends two days ago. People who travelled by wagon." The hunter looked past Mallory to where the wagon remained stationary.

Mallory glanced between the wagoner and the hunter. "He had nothing to do with it. Nor did the half-elf." She didn't want to put anyone else in danger.

The hunter frowned, his expression slowly clearing. "You're protecting them."

Mallory smiled. "Not exactly. They weren't involved so I'm not about to let them take the blame for something we did."

The hunter came closer to her. "My name is

Welby. I'll help you hide the tracks. You can cut the rope."

Mallory crouched at his feet as she drew her dagger. "What do you mean by hide the tracks?"

"A good hunter can read a story in the tracks around them. You confronted the hellions who had killed all but one wolf. A cub." The hunter nodded towards Fang. "There was a fight and the hellions were killed as well as one of your party. Someone with a revive because they respawned a little away from the fight. You took the wolf cub with you after moving the bodies to the side of the road."

Mallory finished cutting through the rope and sheathed her dagger as she rose to her feet. "You can tell that from marks in the dirt?"

He looked at the ground, taking a step to the side as he examined her tracks. "You were the one who revived." He met her gaze. "I'll help you hide your tracks. Anyone who is willing to take on hellions needs all the help they can get."

"Thank you?" She wasn't quite sure what to think. A glance over her shoulder showed Danae kept watch while the rest of the party searched the hellions.

The hunter chuckled. "I don't blame you for being wary." He pointed to a tree at the side of the road with a low thin branch. "Can you cut that off for me? I'll use it for wiping out the tracks."

Mallory broke off the branch, needing to use her dagger to finish separating it from the tree, and handed it to him, remembering once she'd finished the task that they had an axe. She watched as Welby ran the leaves of the branch over the tracks in the area, noticing the journal icon in the corner of her vision. Checking she found it was a new crafting ability. *You have unlocked woodcutter, a crafting ability that allows you to cut various trees and refine the timber.* It didn't take long for her companions to unlock the ability, learning they needed to use a tool to remove a branch and not rely on their hands to break it. They used the axe, handing it around as each took a turn.

After the bodies of the hellions were dumped on the side of the road, Brodie having pointed out they had the same skull tattoos as the previous ones they'd fought, Welby cleared away evidence of the fight. He also followed behind the wagon for a bit, wiping out all the tracks except the wheel ruts and the tracks of the horses pulling it. He even stopped at the location of their previous fight. He asked Danae to ride along the side of the road, leading the donkey. The tough grass would make it harder to notice her passing and it would look like she wasn't part of the wagon group.

Eventually, he told them to stay on the wagon and joined them, wiping away his tracks and tossing the branch far to one side of the road. "That should make it difficult for them to find out who is to blame."

Ryan held out his hand to the hunter, both of them sitting on the top of the chests. "Thank you."

"No, thank you for saving me. Where are you going?"

"Buckneth." Callum held out a sheathed skinning knife, hilt first. "We found this on the hellions and thought it might be yours."

The hunter took the knife. "It is. I thought I'd never see it again." His gaze remained on the knife. "Like I thought I'd never see my home again."

"Where are you from?" Danae asked.

"Wildebay."

"A lot of shapeshifters live there," Danae said.

Welby nodded. "Deer." A wry smile fleetingly appeared. "Which is ironic since I chose to be a hunter." He paused a moment. "I need to get home as soon as possible so I can track down my brother and find out what happened to him." Welby looked at each of them. "Would you be interested in helping me rescue my brother when I find out where they took him?"

Mallory nodded when Ryan looked towards her, smiling when everyone in the group nodded. "Let us know when you find out and we'll see what we can do."

Danae leaned forward. "We're going on to Surith from Buckneth. You could travel with us. It should be safer than travelling alone. Unless the hellions learn it was us that killed their people."

Welby turned to Mallory. "You don't mind?"

She shook her head. "No. Danni is right. It'll be safer to travel together."

"Why can't you turn into a deer to go home?" Brodie asked. "Wouldn't that be faster?"

"I can't remain in that form long enough to travel that distance," Welby said.

The wagoner glanced over his shoulder. "I have friends in Wildebay. If you would join me up the front I'd enjoy hearing how they're doing."

Brodie waited until Welby was seated beside the wagoner before he muttered under his breath. "So much for not talking to anybody."

Laughing, Mallory checked her journal, guessing there was a new quest from both the icon in the corner of her vision and Brodie's comment. She was right. *Captured By Hellions: The hunter from Wildebay and his brother were captured by hellions. He is in need of help to rescue his brother once he learns where he was taken.*

"Maybe I can stay on Ruby Isle a little longer and help out," Danae said. "There's plenty of time before I have to be at the academy." She turned to Brodie, smiling. "By then you might be ready to travel to Merrow too."

"That'd be cool." Brodie turned to Ryan. "Don't you think?"

Callum spoke before Ryan could. "We have to look at the variables, the amount of time it takes to travel there, how often ships sail between each location and what else we need to do."

"Well?" Brodie asked.

Callum snorted. "It's not that quick to calculate. I don't have the information I need." He glanced over his shoulder, in the direction of Wayholt. "What I want to know right now is what the hellion meant by Cape Barren when I mentioned coffee. Does that mean it can be found there? Wherever there is."

"Talking of the hellions." Ryan dropped a silver and two copper pieces into Mallory's hand. "We also got a short sword and a pair of black trousers from them." He grinned. "They're in severe need of washing."

"Can we forget about the unimportant things for now? I need to know about Cape Barren and coffee," Callum said.

"You're going to want to forget about Cape Barren," Danae said.

"Why is that?" Mallory asked.

"It's as far north as you can go, by land, from Eridell." Danae gestured towards the north as she spoke.

"And?" Callum asked.

"It's north of Hellfire." Danae met Callum's gaze. "You've never heard of Hellfire, have you?" She glanced around the group. "None of you have or you wouldn't be so calm."

Callum shook his head. "What is Hellfire?"

"It's worse than it sounds and it doesn't sound all that great a place," Danae said. "It's where demons live. The land two hundred kilometres north and south of the demonic line." When Callum didn't comment she added, "Home of the demonic dark forces."

Ryan chuckled. "Sounds like you need to go through hell and back for coffee if it's to be found up there."

Callum faced his brother. "Whatever it takes. I need my coffee."

Mallory opened her mouth to argue, closing it when she saw how serious Callum was. "Can we try and get seeds from home first?"

Callum stared at Mallory for a moment before he nodded. "One more chance. Then if we need to, we go through hell for my morning coffee."

The wagoner looked over his shoulder. "Must be pretty good if you're willing to go to that sort of effort for it."

"You have no idea," Callum said.

"I might know a few people interested in going into business with you. Ones with farmland and trade contacts," the wagoner said.

"People who could grow the coffee for me?" Callum asked.

"Not exactly for you. It would be a partnership as such," the wagoner said. "Since they'd be providing all the resources except the plant, you'd probably only have a small percentage of the partnership."

Callum grinned. "Which would mean there'd be coffee in the area."

Ryan chuckled. "Sounds like it."

"Stop talking," Brodie muttered. "At this rate, we're going to have a million quests."

Chapter Thirty-Nine

Mallory laughed, looking towards Ryan when he chuckled again. She opened her journal to check out the new quest. *In Search Of Beans: The wagoner from Buckneth has contacts who might be interested in growing coffee shrubs if you can bring seeds or seedlings and the knowledge they would need to produce coffee.*

"Now that sounds like a quest worth doing," Callum said.

Mallory thought of something and moved closer to the front of the wagon, sitting on a chest directly behind the wagon seat. "Where did the hellions come from? The ones we found on the road to Wayholt."

Welby turned to face her. "They have an encampment about twenty minutes north east of where you found us. When their friends didn't return this morning, as expected, they made me track down where they'd been. They were angry to find the bodies. Especially since wild animals had been at them."

Mallory shuddered, wishing he hadn't shared that bit of information. "Are there others at the encampment who can track?"

Welby shook his head. "That's why they came after me and my brother. We're both good at tracking. The ones you took out weren't the first ones to go missing."

"I didn't know hellions were setting up in places this far north. I thought they were mainly in the south west of Ruby Isle. In Cutthroat Harbour and Deadman Cove," Danae said. "It makes me glad I'm moving to Eridell. I wonder if my parents will change their minds and move to Eridell too."

"I hear it's not much better over there," Welby said. "They're everywhere these days."

Mallory noticed the journal icon reappear in the corner of her vision and she grinned when Brodie spoke.

"I told you to stop talking."

She checked her journal, her smile fading as she saw the quest. *Hellions In The North: Notify the law about the hellion encampment or take matters into your own hands.*

"What are we meant to do with all these quests?" Brodie demanded.

"Complete them or ignore them," Ryan said.

Mallory returned to where she was sitting earlier, next to Ryan, leaning against him when he draped his arm around her shoulders. She thought of Danae's earlier words. Cutthroat Harbour and Deadman Cove. The names sounded bad enough without needing to learn more about them. Were they a high enough level to travel to places like that?

The rest of the trip to Buckneth was uneventful and they arrived well before dark. The wagoner pulled up in front of his place and looked over his shoulder. "Should we start our journey to Surith tomorrow morning?"

Mallory smiled and nodded when Ryan looked at her.

When everyone else nodded, Ryan suggested, "After breakfast?"

"Seven-thirty?" the wagoner asked. "We can sort out the details before we leave." He held out a silver coin. "Thank you for getting me safely home to Buckneth."

Ryan nodded. "Where can we put our donkey for the night?"

"I can take her to the sheep farm where I agist

my horses. The shepherd charges two copper pieces a night when it comes to short-term agistments. If you tie her up out the front of the tavern I'll collect her once I unhitch my horses."

Danae held out two copper pieces. "Can Augusta stay there too?"

The wagoner nodded, taking the coins. "Leave her out the front of the tavern."

Mallory glanced around at everyone and when they nodded, she handed over two copper pieces. "Thank you. We'll see you in the morning." She jumped off the wagon, along with the rest of her party.

The wagoner put a hand on Welby's shoulder when he started to move. "You're welcome to stay with me and my wife tonight. It's nothing fancy."

"I'd appreciate that." Welby remained seated. "The hellions took everything I had with me except my clothes."

Danae looked at the sky as the wagoner drove around to the back of his place. "We have about an hour left until dark."

Ryan led the donkey to the front of the tavern. "Mallory and I will organise a room for the night and put our gear in it while the rest of you exchange the herbs for as many cloth bags and sacks as you can. We're going to need them. Danni can stay here tonight and look after Smudge, Fang and the gear while we go home. We can work out what time we need to leave and what time we have to return during our meal."

"Finally. I can go home and have some coffee." Callum opened up the pannier and started filling the basket with herbs, handing the fishing pole he'd been carrying to Ryan.

"You forgot to mention we're also going to have a decent meal." Brodie helped Callum put the herbs in the basket, smiling at Danae when she joined them. "And we can collect our pie in the morning."

It didn't take Mallory and Ryan long to pay for a room and put all their gear and Danae's in it, leaving only the halter and lead rope on the donkey and the bridle and reins on Augusta. They returned upstairs to wait for the rest of their party to return.

Ryan dropped the large, iron key on top of the chest and stretched out on the bed, moving over as far as he could. He grinned up at Mallory who remained standing. "Plenty of space." He patted the bed beside him.

She returned his grin, lying beside him. "Your idea of plenty of space is rather cramped." She brought up her journal, checking the completed quest. *Trading*

Opportunity: The wagoner was relieved to be escorted safely home and grateful for your influence at South Peak Mine that gained him a better trade deal. You were rewarded with one silver piece for your party. You also earned twenty experience points each. She smiled. "Brodie should be happy we got rid of a quest."

Ryan chuckled. "Yeah, but we replaced it with another three."

She laughed softly, her gaze drawn to the door when it opened, the rest of their party entering the room. Turning slightly, she met Ryan's gaze. "Should we stay here so you can have a sleep and regain your health?"

"I didn't think about that." Callum dropped several bags on top of one of the panniers. "Should we stay tonight?"

"No." Ryan glanced at the bags on the pannier. "How many did you get?"

"Four calico bags about half a metre long and thirty centimetres wide and two hessian bags about a metre by half a metre wide and two sacks about half the size of the hessian bags."

"That should do us for a while," Ryan said. "We can sort the food, crockery and other stuff into different bags in the panniers."

"Now?" Callum picked up Smudge who was

leaning against his leg. "I was thinking about taking Smudge to see Ninette before we leave the area. I was also wondering if I could have a gold coin to give her."

"She'll only spend it on something stupid," Brodie said.

"Tell her we have a spare dagger and a short sword if she wants one of them. We can also temporarily let her into our party so she can choose one of those two classes," Ryan said.

"Are you kidding?" Brodie demanded. "That sword is probably worth more than a gold coin."

Ryan answered him with a grin.

"Mallory will need it when she adds the warrior class," Brodie argued.

"We can buy another one. Or might get one from a fight," Ryan said. "But we owe Ninette this. Her father doesn't pay her what she's worth. Do you want to be like him?"

Brodie scowled. "I'm nothing like him."

"You're not coming with me?" Callum asked Ryan.

"I'll have a sleep. Should be able to get in an hour before dinner. That'll bring me back to thirteen health. Enough to get me through the next day."

"You hope." Mallory rose to her feet. "I'll sort out the panniers. Does anyone want to help?"

"I'm going with Callum. So is Danni." Brodie ushered them towards the door.

Danae tried to turn back. "We should help."

"We'll make too much noise and keep Ryan awake." Brodie opened the door, continuing to hurry Danae and Callum outside, Fang following him, Smudge still in Callum's arms.

Ryan chuckled when the door closed. "You can leave it until the morning if you want."

"It's okay. I wouldn't want Callum walking out there alone. It'll be almost dark when he returns." Mallory stared down at Ryan, smiling. "Stop talking and go to sleep."

"You could join me." He patted the space beside him again.

Mallory laughed softly. "You're meant to be sleeping." She turned away from him, ignoring his chuckle as she sorted through their gear. It didn't take her as long as she'd thought and she headed downstairs rather than light the lantern and possibly wake Ryan.

Chapter Forty

Mallory was sitting at a table, writing in her notebook when the rest of the party returned, joining her.

"What are you doing?" Danae leaned closer to peer at the page.

"Keeping track of our days."

"That's a strange way of doing it. Why don't you write the date?" Danae asked.

"The date." Mallory stared at Danae.

"Yes, the date." Danae nodded. "It's the sixth day of the second month of the year five hundred and fourteen."

"Inadon is only five hundred and fourteen years old?" Callum asked.

Danae shook her head. "That's how long people have been keeping track of time. When things became more civilised on Inadon."

"I hate to think what they were like before," Callum said.

"Bad. Really bad if the old stories are true," Danae said.

Mallory wrote the date at the top of her diary entry. "How many months are in a year?" She went back, fixing up the dates for the previous entries.

"Twelve months. Each month ends with the full moon and is only twenty-nine days long. Most areas have four seasons, each season lasting three months. But then that depends on how close you are to the demonic line, which is the hottest part of the world and runs around the middle of it, or how close you are to the far north or far south of the world where it's frozen."

Mallory cleaned the nib of the pen. "The demonic line sounds like the equator."

"What is an equator?" Danae asked.

"The hottest part of our world. The equator is an imaginary line that runs around it," Callum said.

"I wouldn't know if you could call the demonic line imaginary," Danae said. "I mean, you can't see it, but you can feel it. Even out in the ocean. And nowhere along the demonic line, and two hundred kilometres on either side of it, is safe. It's full of all sorts of demons and monsters. Including in the ocean."

Brodie turned to Callum. "I don't think risking our lives is worth coffee."

"Another couple of days, and you'll be risking your life because I don't have coffee," Callum warned.

"I've noticed you use kilometres and kilos. I would have thought everyone'd use miles and pounds," Mallory said.

"My father told me how some adventurers were using kilometres and kilograms about twenty-five years ago and traders were some of the first to start using those measurements due to how much easier it was to calculate things. It wasn't until about eight years ago those measurements became more common," Danae said. "There are still a lot of people who use the old measurements."

Brodie's attention was caught by a plate of food being taken to the neighbouring table. "Think it's time to wake Ryan?"

Mallory checked her journal, pulling up Ryan's stats. He'd regained a health point and was now at thirteen. She glanced at the blackboard behind the bar. The same meals and prices were listed as last time. Stew probably wasn't much of a celebratory meal, even though it was the cheapest option. "Everyone having roast mutton for dinner?" She closed her notebook and returned it, the pen and ink to her satchel.

"And an ale," Brodie said.

"No. That'll bring the meal up to a silver piece. Eight copper pieces is bad enough. You can have water with dinner." Mallory counted out the coins and put them on the table. Forty copper pieces. "Order five roasts. I'll wake Ryan."

"What about Fang and Smudge?" Callum asked.

Mallory placed another two copper pieces on the table. "Order them a stew to share. I won't get through all my roast so they can have some of it too." She headed upstairs, ignoring Brodie's protests that she should order another bowl of stew because he'd eat the rest of her roast.

Ryan opened the door as she reached it. He grinned. "Good timing." He slid his arms around her waist, drawing her close. "How long have we got until dinner is ready?" His lips met hers before she could answer.

Eventually she drew back, smiling. "They were ordering it when I came upstairs. We shouldn't be too long because Brodie was already talking about wanting my dinner when I was heading up here."

Chuckling, Ryan kept one arm around her waist,

locking the door before he headed for the stairs. "That doesn't surprise me."

As they walked down the stairs, Mallory told Ryan about the conversation she'd had with Danae regarding dates on Inadon, the demonic line and measurements. They arrived at the table seconds before the food.

Ryan sat beside Mallory, turning his attention to Callum. "What did Ninette say?"

"That she'd think about it and let us know before we left in the morning," Callum said.

"Okay." Ryan picked up his cutlery. "It's good she wants to think about it and not jump into it."

Throughout the meal they talked over the logistics of returning. Brodie wanted to come back that night, but Callum pointed out it wasn't enough time. Barely any would have passed. Ryan suggested leaving during the morning from their world so they weren't tired from lack of sleep when they reached Inadon. When Mallory refused to let him scribble in her notebook, Callum drew in the gravy on his plate, trying to calculate the times.

Brodie stared at the plate, slowly shaking his head. "What a waste."

Mallory didn't bother trying to stop the laughter that bubbled up, ignoring the glare her brother sent her way. "How are we meant to leave of a morning during the week? We have school and leave home before our parents do."

"I could borrow a van from one of my mates and pick you up at the corner when you head to the bus stop. There should be more than enough time to park somewhere out of the way and use my laptop for the disc." Ryan grinned. "He has curtains over the windows in the back so there'd be privacy to get changed."

"Why does he have curtains?" Brodie asked.

Mallory held up a hand when Ryan started to speak. "I don't want to know why he has curtains in his van. Seriously. Do not want to know at all."

Ryan chuckled, turning to his brother. "We need to be back here by about seven tomorrow morning to give us time to get geared up. The earliest we'll be able to leave home on a weekday morning is eight. That should give us enough time for the three of you to go to school when we return. I can drop all of you off since that'll take a lot less time than going by bus."

Brodie leaned closer to Callum. "What did you figure out? When are we coming back? Are you going to eat that gravy when you're finished?"

"I need to know what the time is now," Callum said. "Otherwise I'm guessing."

"I'll ask Ahron." Brodie dashed over to the bar, leaning against it as he waited his turn to talk. He was back in less than a minute. "Almost seven."

Callum made more calculations in the gravy, muttering under his breath. He smeared some of them and started again, continuing to mutter. Eventually, he looked up. "If we leave here tonight at twenty-five minutes to midnight we can leave our world eight o'clock Monday morning. Ryan can borrow his mate's van. That will get us back here at six-thirty tomorrow morning."

"How will we know when it's twenty-five minutes to midnight?" Brodie asked.

"You'll have to keep asking Ahron." Ryan grinned. "You never know, he might get fed up with you asking and let you borrow his pocket watch until midnight. Danni can return it to him."

"What are we going to do while we wait?" Brodie asked.

"Ryan should sleep so he can gain more health," Mallory said.

"I was thinking of washing those new trousers and the clothes we're leaving behind so we've got something clean to come back to," Ryan said.

Mallory rose from the table. "You go sleep and the rest of us will sort out the washing."

They strung up a line before they went to wash the clothes, everyone changing out of the clothes they were leaving behind, brushing the knots from their hair and tidying themselves. Even Danae changed into fresh clothes so she could wash hers. Another pair of black trousers and this time a dark blue blouse.

They took the clothes down to the well, borrowing a timber bucket from Ahron to wash the garments in. Brodie and Callum seemed to end up with more water on them than necessary. Mallory slowly shook her head. "How are we going to explain that to Mum if you're wet when we go home?" She'd moved the lantern further away from the well, worried it would be knocked over from their antics.

Brodie grinned. "We had a water fight?"

Once the clothes were washed and rung out as much as possible, Mallory and Danae headed upstairs to hang them over the rope, neither trusting Brodie and Callum not to wake Ryan. Once the clothes were hung up, the four of them sat at the table they'd eaten their dinner at, talking over some of the quests they'd completed and which ones they should do next. After Danae and the wagoner had been taken to Surith.

Brodie glanced at the bar again. "Can I have two copper coins? I'll share the ale with Callum."

"No." Mallory sighed heavily, annoyed by how

many times he'd asked that question. "Mum would never let us visit Ryan and Callum again if you came home from their place smelling like alcohol."

Callum laughed. "It'd be worse than that. She wouldn't let us visit your place either. I'm sure she's looking for an excuse to say you can't date Ryan."

"Parents tend to be like that." Danae laughed softly before launching into her own tale of problems her father had caused when it came to deciding who she could associate with. And the things she'd needed to do to get around his orders.

Mallory kept an eye on Ryan's health, checking the journal regularly. Once he had four health points back, she woke him, convincing him to drink two cups of health tea before they went downstairs. It was an effort for him. With no way to tell the time, Brodie kept asking Ahron until he handed over the pocket watch, telling Brodie that Danae better bring it back as soon as they left.

They headed upstairs to the room when it was twenty-five past eleven. Danae looked at each of them. "Are you sure you'll be back in the morning? Nothing will go wrong?"

"I worked it all out. We'll be back here at six-thirty," Callum said.

Brodie handed the pocket watch to Danae. "Make sure you give this to Ahron as soon as we go."

"I will." Danae leaned close and kissed Brodie on each cheek, smiling at him. "I'll see you in the morning."

Brodie stared at her, open-mouthed.

Mallory struggled not to smile at his expression. But it was difficult. She slipped her hand in Ryan's. "Ready?"

Ryan nodded.

Chapter Forty-One

Mallory closed her eyes, thinking over the commands before she spoke them. "Leave party member Danae behind. Leave party member Smudge behind. Leave party member Fang behind. Save progress and transfer party home." The world went black, sounds, smells and sensations fading, returning again seconds later. Her gaze scanned Ryan's room. She felt out of place. Like Inadon was her home. Not this world.

Callum stared at the floor. "All the coffee is where I was standing. Not a single bit missing."

"I want to go back already," Ryan said.

Mallory momentarily tightened her grip on his hand. "Me too." Her phone beeped and she glanced at her backpack she'd put it in.

"It was good to return to Buckneth," Ryan said.

"Don't we want to leave that place behind?" Brodie asked.

"Being back there feels like we're about to work on a main quest again," Callum said.

Ryan gave a single nod. "Exactly."

Brodie sat on the floor and picked up the packet of chips he'd opened before they'd left. "What did we get paid and what superhero stuff did we do?"

Mallory let go of Ryan's hand, reaching for her backpack. "Wayholt and South Peak Mine did feel like side quests. Not that there's anything wrong with side quests." Her phone beeped again. "I wonder who the second message is from." She found her phone, taking it out of the backpack, her frown deepening. "They're both from the guardians."

"Do you think we're in trouble for not doing the quest they asked us to do?" Callum asked.

Mallory checked the first message, reading it aloud. "Good Samaritans came to the rescue of a man who was mugged, homeowner with unsolvable pest problem finally learns the cause, due to an anonymous tip a local gang is brought to justice, kidnapping solved due to unexpected help, convenience store robbery prevented by an unlikely group."

"We're not an unlikely group," Brodie protested.

"We only managed to do five quests this time," Callum said.

"What's the other message?" Ryan asked.

Mallory's stomach somersaulted as she opened it. For a second the words made no sense. "Do you want your bounties for directly taking down members of the dark forces paid into the same accounts your quest bonuses are paid into? You will receive ten dollars per level per dark forces member and fifty dollars per poppet handed in to be unbound." She looked up from her phone. "We get paid for going after members of the dark forces."

Brodie victory punched the air. "Hell yeah. We're superheroes and bounty hunters."

Mallory glanced at each of them. "That's a yes?" When they nodded, she sent off the reply, one returning almost instantly. "Payment of two gold pieces and six silver pieces for Danae of Simria has been deposited into the Inadon International Bank. Temporary code to access the account is three thousand eight hundred and seventy-two. A new code will need to be set upon initial access."

"Splitting our earnings between five isn't good when we've done one less quest than last time. Lucky we got the extra hundred and fifty from taking out the five level-three hellions," Callum said. "I'm not sure if the amount paid on Inadon is as good as what is paid here."

"We need to hand in that poppet." Brodie grabbed out a handful of chips. "We'll get paid in both worlds for it."

Mallory slipped her phone into her pocket. "Monday is ages away." She checked the purple notebook she'd left on Ryan's bed. It seemed like such a long time ago that she'd written the words.

Ryan took the disc out of the laptop and put it back in the case, handing it to Mallory. "We could make some clothes to take with us."

Mallory returned the disc to her backpack, sitting on the bed to remove her boots. "We'll probably be better off buying them. We can't make anything like the ones people are wearing on Ruby Isle. We've looked out of place long enough. I'll sell the mage robe and we can buy more gear. And we need to get armour. Something to help us survive those higher level creatures and hellions."

Callum sat in front of Ryan's laptop. "We need to head to the mainland. We're doing too many things on Ruby Isle and not making enough connections in the area we plan to stay."

"We keep saying we're better off moving to Eridell, but what if we aren't?" Mallory asked. "What if staying on the island is a better idea? Danni's father moved from Eridell because he could earn more on Ruby Isle."

"It's too small," Brodie said. "Besides, Danni is leaving Ruby Isle so it can't be that great."

Callum looked up from the screen of the laptop. "I found somewhere we can buy coffee plant seeds. It's only a couple of hours away. I sent them a message to see if we can buy them tomorrow."

Ryan chuckled. "And I'm guessing you're expecting me to drive you there."

Callum stood up, glancing at the door. "Do you think Mum and Dad have gone to the shops yet? I'm dying for a coffee."

Ryan shrugged.

"Too bad. I can't wait any longer." Callum strode from the room, closing the door behind him.

The rest of the afternoon, they spent discussing their various options, Brodie checking his bank account and grinning when he found a hundred and thirty dollars already in his account. They tried ringing Kern and Ewen, but the call went to their message bank.

As it grew dark, Ryan walked Mallory out the front, standing on the patio with his arms wrapped around her waist. "Want to come for a drive with us tomorrow? If we're lucky, we'll be able to take some seeds back and not have to worry about going through hell for coffee."

Mallory laughed. "I've got a feeling we're not that lucky. We need to get better organised in both worlds. We keep talking about needing a base on Inadon, we pretty much need one here too. I'm dying for a shower, but I can't exactly go home and have one or Mum will want to know what's going on."

Ryan chuckled. "I bet she'd jump to the wrong conclusion. You could have had a shower here when my parents went to the shop."

"And put the same clothes back on? No thanks."

Brodie came outside. "You ready?"

"Almost." Mallory kissed Ryan before she let him go.

He tugged her back. "Let me know if you can come with us tomorrow."

"Okay. Will do."

They were barely in the front door before Norine said, "The pair of you reek of sweat. What have you been doing?"

Brodie brandished an imaginary stiletto. "Destroying the dark forces, killing goblins, rescuing a wolf cub and travelling around looking for quests."

"Showers. Both of you. I'm starting dinner shortly." Norine headed for the kitchen, stopping when her phone rang. She returned to the lounge room and answered it.

Mallory waited until their mum had wandered down the hallway, talking on the phone, and shut herself in her room before she spoke. "Destroying the dark forces?" She grinned.

"Well, we did." Brodie looked from Mallory to the hallway. "I'm having a shower first." He took off down the hallway at a run.

She glared after him, striding to her room when the bathroom door slammed shut. After she had a chance to shower, she came out to find her brother in the kitchen, cooking. "That actually smells good."

Brodie nodded. "The kitchen seems more familiar now. Or at least cooking does."

Mallory stared at her brother as if she'd never seen him before. "How strange."

Norine came into the kitchen. She stared at Brodie silently for a moment. "Who are you and what have you done with my son? How did you go from barely making sandwiches to cooking a meal overnight?"

Brodie turned off the elements on the stovetop and began to dish up the food. "I forgot to mention I levelled up my cooking while I was doing all that questing and hunting down the dark forces."

Norine slowly shook her head, opening her mouth several times, saying nothing.

Mallory grinned, meeting her brother's gaze. "Imagine what you could do at level a hundred if this is level three."

Norine took the plate Brodie gave her. "Do you think we can have one meal that doesn't include discussing a computer game?" She headed to the table.

Brodie handed Mallory a plate of food. "I'm more interested in knowing what levelling up rogue, mage, warrior and archer to thirty will do."

Mallory stared at him a moment, the excitement in his eyes echoing how she felt. "Let's find out." She returned his grin, counting down the hours until they could return to Inadon. Next time she wanted to gain a character level. And find out about a fire drake nest. She couldn't wait to get started.

Final Stats

Character weight does not include any backpacks, satchels, their contents or items carried by livestock.

Mallory

Character Level: 0
Health: 15
Stamina: 25
Mana: 35
Weight: 3kg 50g/40kg

CAS XP: 35/105
Available CAS Points: 3
Available Class Points: 0
Level Progress: 7/10

Attributes

Strength: 4
Constitution: 5
Intelligence: 7
Wisdom: 7

Dexterity: 5
Charisma: 5
Luck: 5

Class

Mage: 0

Class Skills
None

Spells

Level 0
Fireball: 0
Mana cost: 3
Cooldown: 2 seconds
Damage: low 3, normal 5, critical 7
Duration: Instant

Weapon and Armour Affinity

Cloth Armour: 0
Dagger: 1 (+1% damage)
Wand: 1 (+1% damage)

Crafting

Alchemy: 1	Husbandry: 0
Bard: 0	Languages: 0
Bartering: 0	Scribe: 0
Cooking: 0	Wheelwright: 1
Fishing: 0	Woodcutter: 0
Hunting: 0	

Reputation

Global: 0
Local Areas:
Ruby Isle: Buckneth 20,
South Peak Mine 5, Wayholt 4.

Buffs and Negative Stats

None

Available Revives 0

Ryan

Character Level: 0
Health: 19/21
Stamina: 35
Mana: 20
Weight: 9kg 640g/70kg

CAS XP: 30/105
Available CAS Points: 0
Available Class Points: 0
Level Progress: 7/10

Attributes

Strength: 7
Constitution: 7
Intelligence: 5
Wisdom: 4

Dexterity: 5
Charisma: 5
Luck: 5

Class

Warrior: 0

Class Skills
None

Spells

None

Weapon and Armour Affinity

Chain Mail Armour: 0
Short Sword: 1 (+1% damage)
Shield: 1 (+1% damage)
(-1% damage taken)

Crafting

Alchemy: 0
Bard: 0
Bartering: 0
Cooking: 0
Fishing: 0
Hunting: 4

Husbandry: 0
Languages: 0
Scribe: 0
Wheelwright: 1
Woodcutter: 0

Reputation

Global: 0
Local Areas:
Ruby Isle: Buckneth 20,
South Peak Mine 5, Wayholt 4 .

Buffs and Negative Stats

None

Available Revives 1

Bradie

Character Level: 0
Health: 15
Stamina: 25
Mana: 25
Weight: 4kg 380g/50kg

CAS XP: 36/105
Available CAS Points: 0
Available Class Points: 0
Level Progress: 7/10

Attributes

Strength: 5
Constitution: 5
Intelligence: 4
Wisdom: 5

Dexterity: 7
Charisma: 7
Luck: 5

Class

Rogue: 0

Class Skills
None

Spells

None

Weapon and Armour Affinity

Stiletto: 1 (+1% damage)
Throwing Knives: 1 (+1% damage)
Leather Armour: 0

Crafting

Alchemy: 0
Bard: 0
Bartering: 1
Cooking: 3
Fishing: 0
Hunting: 0

Husbandry: 0
Languages: 0
Scribe: 0
Wheelwright: 1
Woodcutter: 0

Reputation

Global: 0
Local Areas:
Ruby Isle: Buckneth 20,
South Peak Mine 5, Wayholt 4 .

Buffs and Negative Stats

None

Available Revives 0

Callum

Character Level: 0
Health: 15
Stamina: 25
Mana: 25
Weight: 5kg 80g/50kg

CAS XP: 36/105
Available CAS Points: 4
Available Class Points: 0
Level Progress: 7/10

Attributes

Strength: 5
Constitution: 5
Intelligence: 5
Wisdom: 5

Dexterity: 7
Charisma: 4
Luck: 7

Class

Archer: 0

Class Skills
None

Spells

None

Weapon and Armour Affinity

Short Bow 1 (+1% damage)
Hunting Knife: 1 (+1% damage)
Studded Leather Armour: 0

Crafting

Alchemy: 0
Bard: 0
Bartering: 0
Cooking: 0
Fishing: 0
Hunting: 0

Husbandry: 0
Languages: 0
Scribe: 0
Wheelwright: 1
Woodcutter: 0

Reputation

Global: 0
Local Areas:
Ruby Isle: Buckneth 20,
South Peak Mine 5, Wayholt 4 .

Buffs and Negative Stats

None

Available Revives 1

Danae

Character Level: 1
Health: 21
Stamina: 35
Mana: 25
Weight: 4kg 932g/60kg

CAS XP: 51/110
Available CAS Points: 2
Available Class Points: 0
Level Progress: 2/10

Attributes

Strength: 6
Constitution: 7
Intelligence: 5
Wisdom: 5

Dexterity: 9
Charisma: 4
Luck: 7

Class

Archer: 1

Class Skills
None

Spells

None

Weapon and Armour Affinity

Short Bow: 1 (+1% damage)
Hunting Knife: 1 (+1% damage)
Studded Leather: 0
Sling: 0
Slingshot
Unarmed: 1 (+1% damage)

Crafting

Alchemy: 3	Glassblowing: 1
Bartering: 1	Languages: 0
Clothier: 0	Scribe: 0
Cooking: 1	Wheelwright: 1
Fishing: 0	Woodcutter: 0

Reputation

Global: 0
Local Areas:
Ruby Isle: Buckneth 2, Simria 22,
South Peak Mine 5, Ursen 0,
Wayholt 12 .

Buffs and Negative Stats

None

Racial Bonus

Archer +10% damage
Mage capable of using spells
one level above class level

Available Revives 1

COMPANION ANIMALS' FINAL STATS

Smudge 8HP (Callum)

232XP/1000XP

Fang 6HP (Brodie)

211XP/1000XP

Free Ebook

Subscribe to Avril's newsletter and receive a free ebook. This ebook is exclusive to those on her mailing list. To find out more about this offer visit:

www.avrilsabine.com/free-ebook

*

We value your privacy and will not sell, rent, exchange or loan your email address to third parties. Your information is confidential and you are under no obligation to remain on the mailing list and can unsubscribe at any time.

Acknowledgements

Once again, thanks to the usual crew and a special thanks to our early readers. Your feedback is certainly appreciated.

To The Reader

If you enjoyed this book, why not consider leaving a review to help other readers discover it too? Reader engagement is one of the few ways that lets an author know readers want more books in a particular series or genre. So leave a review and tell friends, not only about this book but also about other ones you've enjoyed, so you can continue to enjoy books by your favourite authors for years to come.

Dreams are meant to be lived,

Avril, Storm and Rhys.

About The Authors

Avril is an Australian author who lives with her family on acreage in South East Queensland. She writes mostly young adult and children's speculative fiction, but has been known to dabble in other genres. You can find more information about her at www.avrilsabine.com where you can also subscribe to her newsletter to be kept informed about new releases, current projects, blog posts and exclusive news.

Storm has a wide range of interests from gaming and blacksmithing to cooking and sewing. It's not unusual to find him cooking at any hour of the day or night, particularly after a long gaming session.

Rhys loves books and gaming and has thoroughly enjoyed combining two of his favourite things. He has been running tabletop gaming sessions for the past few years and enjoys creating characters and doing in depth worldbuilding.

Titles By Avril Sabine

Stories about strong characters and characters who discover their strengths.

SERIES

Assassins Of The Dead- Young Adult Fantasy/ Paranormal

Book 1: Dark Blade

Book 2: Dragon Touched

Book 3: Society Against Vampires

Book 4: King's Request

Book 5: Duke's Courier

Book 6: Necromancer Resistance

Dragon Blood- Young Adult Urban Fantasy (with elements of romance)

(5 book series)

Book 1: Pliethin

Book 2: Wyvern

Book 3: Surety

Book 4: Knight

Book 5: Mage

Dragon Mage- Young Adult Urban Fantasy (with elements of romance)

(Series two of Dragon Blood series)

Book 1: Promise

Dragon Blood Chronicles- Young Adult Urban Fantasy (with elements of romance)

(Companion stand alone series to Dragon Blood)

Book 1: Oath

Book 2: Betrayed

Guardians Of The Round Table- Young Adult Fantasy LitRPG

(Co-written with Storm and Rhys Petersen)

Book 1: Dexterity Fail

Book 2: Goblin Boots

Book 3: Singed Feathers

Book 4: Frog Mage

Book 5: Crystal Mine

Book 6: Cursed Harp

Rosie's Rangers- Young Adult Western Steampunk

(6 book series)

Book 1: Justice

Book 2: Vengeance

Book 3: Treachery

Book 4: Accused

Book 5: Wanted

Book 6: Corruption

Mark Of Kings- Children's Fantasy

(Upper middle grade/preteen)

(4 book series)

Book 1: The Arena

Book 2: The Island

Book 3: The Assassin

Book 4: The King

STAND ALONE SERIES

Demon Hunters- Young Adult Urban Fantasy/ Horror (with elements of romance)

Book 1: Blood Sacrifice

Book 2: Retribution

Book 3: Tainted

Book 4: Premonition

Book 5: Cursed

Book 6: Feud

Book 7: Extrication

Plea Of The Damned- Young Adult Urban Fantasy/Paranormal

(6 book series)

Book 1: Forgive Me Lucy

Book 2: Forgive Me Aiden

Book 3: Forgive Me Jena

Book 4: Forgive Me Kobe

Book 5: Forgive Me Marti

Book 6: Forgive Me Dawson

*Realms Of The Fae- Young Adult Urban Fantasy
(with elements of romance)*

The Sword (short story in Like A Girl Anthology)

Heart Of Stone

Book 1: A Debt Owed

Book 2: Marked By The Hunt

Book 3: The Magic Collector

Book 4: An Unexpected Betrayal

Book 5: Imprisoned By Iron

Fairytales Retold (Short Stories)

Snow-White And Rose-Red

The Twelve Brothers

The Light Princess

Beauty And The Beast

Sleeping Beauty

Aschenputtel

The Golden Bird

The Frog Prince

The Death Of Koshchei The Deathless

Myths And Legends Retold (Short Stories)

Ion, Son Of Apollo

Sir Gawain And The Maid With The Narrow Sleeves

Princess Ilse, The Giant's Daughter

YOUNG ADULT NOVELS

Young Adult Fantasy (with elements of romance)

Elf Sight

Earth Bound

Young Adult Urban Fantasy

Stone Warrior (with elements of romance)

The Jungle Inside

Young Adult Contemporary (with elements of romance)

Through Your Eyes

The Ugly Stepsister

Perfect Little Princess

Young Adult Contemporary/Paranormal

Whispers In The Dark (with elements of romance and same sex relationships)

Over Too Soon (with elements of romance)

Young Adult Sci-Fi

Experiment X-One-Six (Urban Sci-Fi/Superheroes)

An Endless Dawn (Post Apocalyptic Sci-Fi)

CHILDREN'S BOOKS

Dragon Lord (Preteen/early teens) (Fantasy)

The Irish Wizard (Upper middle grade) (Urban Fantasy)

SHORT STORIES

Urban Fantasy

Eternally Late

Dealings With Joe

Glimpses (short story in That Moment When Anthology)

Contemporary

The Brat Next Door

Fantasy LitRPG

(Set in the same world as Guardians Of The Round Table Series)

Tales Of Inadon 1: The Disc (Co-written with Storm and Rhys Petersen) (short story in Game On! Anthology)

Post Apocalyptic Sci-Fi

Compulsive Directive

NONFICTION

A Year Of Weekly Writing Exercises (Creative Writing)

Cooking For Families With Allergies (Cooking) (Co-written with Storm Petersen)

Tell Me A Story, Grandma (Memoir)

For the most up to date details on available titles visit:

www.avrilsabine.com/books/bibliography

Guardians Of The Round Table Series

To learn more about this series visit:

www.avrilsabine.com/series/gotrt

Find maps, more stats and details about the next book.

BOOKS AVAILABLE IN THE GUARDIANS OF THE ROUND TABLE SERIES

Book 1: Dexterity Fail

Book 2: Goblin Boots

Book 3: Singed Feathers

Book 4: Frog Mage

Book 5: Crystal Mine

Book 6: Cursed Harp

Book 7: Treasure Seeker

Book 8: Bard's Hollow

BOOKS SET IN THE SAME WORLD AS THE GUARDIANS OF THE ROUND TABLE SERIES

Adventurers Guild Handbook (Lore Book)

Legend Of The Ancestral King (Lore Book)

Lost And Powerful: Myths Of Misplaced Staves (Lore Book)

Disclaimer

This is a work of fiction. Names, characters, businesses, places, events and incidents are either the products of the author's imagination or used in a fictitious manner. Any resemblance to actual persons, living or dead, or actual events is purely coincidental. The opinions expressed or beliefs held are those of the characters and should not be assumed to be the opinions or beliefs of the authors.